D0869158

APOLLO

Bosnian Chronicle | Ivo Andrić

Now in November | Josephine Johnson

The Stone Angel | Margaret Laurence

The Lost Europeans | Emanuel Litvinoff

The Case of Charles Dexter Ward | H.P. Lovecraft

The Nebuly Coat | John Meade Falkner

The Authentic Death of Hendry Jones | Charles Neider

The Hungry Grass | Richard Power

The Man on a Donkey | H.F.M. Prescott

The History of a Town | M.E. Saltykov-Shchedrin

The Day of Judgment | Salvatore Satta

My Son, My Son | Howard Spring

The Man Who Loved Children | Christina Stead

Delta Wedding | Eudora Welty

Heaven's My Destination | Thornton Wilder

The Council of Egypt

Leonardo Sciascia

Translated from the Italian
by Adrienne Foulke

△
APOLLO

Apollo Librarian | Michael Schmidt || Series Editor | Neil Belton
Text Design | Lindsay Nash || Artwork | Jessie Price

www.apollo-classics.com | www.headofzeus.com

First published in Italy as *Il Consiglio d'Egitto* in 1963 by
Giulio Einaudi editore.

First published in English in 1966.

This paperback edition published in the United Kingdom in 2016
by Apollo, an imprint of Head of Zeus Ltd.

1 3 5 7 9 10 8 6 4 2

A CIP catalogue record for this book is available
from the British Library.

ISBN (PB) 9781784978037
      (E) 9781784978020

Typeset by Adrian McLaughlin
Printed and bound in Denmark by Nørhaven

Head of Zeus Ltd
Clerkenwell House
45–47 Clerkenwell Green
London EC1R 0HT

The Council of Egypt

Introduction

In 1783 Sicily was struck by volcanic eruptions, earthquakes and tidal waves, the worst in its history. Leonardo Sciascia ignores this spectacular seismology in *The Council of Egypt*, set like so many of his novels in Palermo, and dealing with the political and moral corruption of a society stifled for more than two millennia ('the obscure, immutable centuries') by a succession of foreign oppressors, millennia which have made Sicilians great deceivers and illusionists. While they seem to accept domination, they shape it to their individual advantage.

In *The Leopard*, Sicily's greatest novel, published in 1958, Giuseppe Tomasi di Lampedusa's Prince boldly enunciates the conservative axiom: 'We must change to stay the same'. Sciascia, with very different politics, is Lampedusa's eloquent and radical heir. His chosen genre is the detective novel with its slow and telling disclosures, but in Sciascia's hands the detective often dies before the crime is solved. In that sense, the author is a truth-teller: pessimistic but plausible.

The Council of Egypt is a historical detective story. More than that, it is a political fable – Sciascia's hardest and wittiest. Published in 1963 when the author was forty-two years old,

Sciascia was a schoolteacher, journalist, communist, an amateur scholar of the great Sicilian playwright Pirandello, a short-story writer and an emerging novelist. His first major novel, *The Day of the Owl*, had appeared two years earlier.

The action begins in something like a historical 1783. The Moroccan ambassador to the Court of Naples, returning to Africa, is shipwrecked on the Sicilian coast. He is entertained by the Viceroy of Sicily, who employs a poor Maltese monk as interpreter, imagining him to be proficient in Arabic. The priest grows in fame and, when the Ambassador puts to sea again, is asked to translate an ancient codex – a relic of the years of Moorish occupation – from the Arabic.

The Sicilian prelate, Monsignor Airoldi, commissions the work from the penniless Benedictine Giuseppe Vella. Hitherto he has made his living as a chaplain of the Order of Malta and a numerist – assigning numbers to the figures in people's dreams in order to 'interpret' them. Vella has only rudimentary Arabic, but seeing a chance to change his circumstances for good, he obliges. Here begins his career as a forger, and also as a highly effective storyteller. 'This is the lie that tells the truth', the poet says. The truth Sciascia explores is not what is written in the ancient codex, but what is revealed in how people respond to Vella's translations and inventions, his spurious, but initially unchallenged, authority. The Abbot's forgery, laced with sufficient fact to fool the antiquarian Monsignor, illuminates the larger picture of Sicily at a time when the forces of change, notably the French Revolution, are quietly becoming irresistible.

The characters, events and families the forgery describes

are drawn from history. The principled and progressive viceroy of the Two Sicilies, Dominico Caracciolo, is also based on an actual historical figure. He proposes reforms to the feudal order, but comes up against the hardening opposition of reactionary forces. The stolid barons and their church block the way. *The Council of Egypt* is the story of their obduracy and its unmasking.

Caracciolo, with his 'Voltairean nose' poking into every corner of Sicilian life, was in fact a great letter-writer, and Sciascia finds his way into the period by means of the immediacy and candour of Caracciolo's writings. Caracciolo's pursuit of corruption, his impatience with the feuding and shuffling for advantage of the island's aristocracy, were Sciascia's timeless subject. He saw in Caracciolo's struggle a modern struggle: that of Sicily emerging from fascism yet still in the grips of the dark forces that held it in thrall for centuries.

The Council is Sciascia's most experimental novel; it is also his most European, touching as it does on the contest between the forces of reform and reaction re-emerging after the temporary defeat of authoritarianism in the wake of the Second World War. Remote yet familiar: the fate of late eighteenth-century Sicily and Sciascia's contemporary Sicily, are both in thrall to corruption, crime and the mafia. Wider, European correspondences can be drawn: the period of writing was, after all, the radical 1960s which did so much to undermine the settled privileges of the post-war establishment in Europe and further afield.

In 1783, foreign books already have an unsettling presence

in Sicily: the ladies are kept, and controlled, by their husbands, but secretly they let themselves loose on French novels that teach them the arts of indiscretion. *The Council* is about the power of writing in a superstitious, repressed, half-literate society. Scripture has undisputed authority, and those who interpret it have power. Abbot Giuseppe Vella, Sciascia's protagonist, an outsider, Maltese by origin, avaricious and scheming, brings a celibate malice to bear on a society that exploits him as confessor and pardoner. Can he achieve the lavish security of an aristocrat, without aristocratic qualities or gifts of his own? He also partakes of the experimental spirit of the late eighteenth century. His darker calculation: can he unmask his corrupt patrons, and lay bare what is concealed beneath the pomp and pedigree that feed off the common man?

With a novelist's creativity, Abbot Vella 'translates' what his patrons believe is an old Arabic chronicle, *The Council of Egypt*. No one can decipher the script in which *The Council* is written. The Abbot pretends to understand it and gradually discloses what this written authority says about privileges, the different families' relative prominence, and the sovereignty over Sicily of the Kingdom of Naples. The world may seem ripe for reform, but his forgery exposes the entrenched resistance of the aristocracy. He divides the powerful and controls them. They court, flatter and enrich him. He becomes a falsifying champion of the old (dis)order, the feudal elite. None of his foes can defeat him until his forgery is suspected and then exposed. Even then truth is resisted. The terrible consequences of intended reform for the reformers themselves are made clear in the novel's violent climax: the execution of a good man and the final imprisonment of the impenitent forger, for whom forgery has become an experiment in the power of language and lies. Sciasica's tone is cool, unsentimental and as uncompromising as his master Stendhal's. In depicting a country, its people and traditions, this is Sciascia's most vivid canvas.

Francesco Paolo Di Blasi, a nobleman with humanist and liberal instincts, is Vella's articulate ally and then his foil. His authority is no match for the Abbot's, who gathers behind him an establishment threatened by modern trends and by change coming from Europe that they will resist at all costs. Both men know that the truth is relative: it can be reshaped, traded, devalued. It is not a force but a kind of currency, a form of fiction to be made and unmade. The tortures to which Di Blasi is subjected are elaborately, infernally cruel. However, his nobility, his resistance to the humiliation he is subjected to, are heroic in quite another key. Here the disciple of Voltaire, of Liberty, makes his accommodations with history. He dies, a hero of sorts, while Vella is consigned to a dungeon.

Sciascia is Sicily's ironic, unforgiving chronicler. He also loves the country, its landscapes and cityscapes, and his writing evokes the place with an unconditional and – again – unsentimental devotion. In the end he admires Vella and lets him triumph in his art: 'the writer in him had shaken off the hand of the imposter and broken free; like one of those shining, black, mettlesome Maltese horses, the writer was off at a gallop, dragging the imposter behind in the dust, his foot caught in the stirrup'. History may be an imposture composed by, and for, the ruling class; this 'parody of a crime', *The Council of Egypt*, is the imposture that pulls back the curtain on that larger, more destructive and disabling imposture. It reveals human nature for what it is: avaricious, controlling, cruel, and yet capable of great invention.

This is a fable, Sciascia himself makes clear, like one of Aesop's, but the fox, the gullible ass and the stolid ox are translated back into the human forms from which they were originally abstracted. Towards the end of the novel, Sciascia indulges in a sweeping prolepsis, reflecting on what Vella might have felt had he experienced the lowest points of the twentieth-century's tragic history; had he seen what human agency was capable of in the Second World War. Vella is spared this revelation, but he is in fact 'struck by dismay at the sudden idea that the world of truth might be here and now, in the world of living men, of history, of books,' – this, after he has spent the best part of his life as a paid interpreter of common people's dreams and a forger.

The Council of Egypt belongs with Pirandello's plays and *The Leopard* among the classics of Sicilian, and Italian, writing – a literature of the uncommon man.

Michael Schmidt, 2016

*We can see [Sicily] from here, the way you can look from the Tuileries
across to the Faubourg Saint-Germain; the Strait — my word,
it's scarcely any wider than that, and yet we are in difficulties over
the crossing. Would you believe it? If all we lacked were a good wind,
we could do as Agamemnon did, and sacrifice a young maiden.
We have more than enough of them, thank God. But there's not a
boat to be had, that's the dilemma. One will be coming in, they say;
so long as I have hopes of this, never suppose, Madame, that I will
cast a single backward glance toward the country where you live, much
as I delight in it. Now I want to see the homeland of Persephone,
and discover why the Devil took himself a wife in that country.*
—COURIER, *Lettres de France et d'Italie*

Part One

Chapter I

The Benedictine whisked a brush of multicolored feathers over the top of the book, puffed out his plump cheeks like the god of winds in an old nautical map, blew black dust from the leather cover, and, with a shiver of what in the circumstances seemed delicate trepidation, laid the volume open on the table. The light fell slantingly from a high window onto the yellowed page, so that the dim characters stood out like a grotesque army of crushed dry black ants. His Excellency Abdallah Mohammed ben-Olman leaned down to study them; his eyes, habitually languid, weary, incurious, were now sharp and alert. He straightened up after a moment, reached under his redingote with his right hand, and drew forth a magnifying glass; the frame and handle were of gold, with green stones so set that the glass seemed a cluster of flowers or fruit on a slender stem.

"'The icebound brook,'" he said, displaying the glass. He smiled, for he had intended to compliment his hosts by quoting the Sicilian poet Ibn Hamdis. Except for Don Giuseppe Vella, however, no one present understood any Arabic, and Don Giuseppe was not qualified to grasp His Excellency's amiable intent in making the quotation, or even qualified to realize that it was a matter of quotation. Therefore, he translated not the words but the gesture – "The glass, he needs the glass" – which Monsignor Airoldi, who was eagerly awaiting His Excellency's pronouncement on the codex, had perfectly well understood.

His Excellency bent over the book again, moving his glass across the page in a tracery of slow ellipses. Don Giuseppe could see the signs leap up into the glass, but they unraveled and sank back onto the worn page before he could decipher them.

His Excellency turned the page, and again he lingered over his examination. He murmured something to himself. He leafed through more pages, scanning them rapidly through his glass, until he came to the last, which swarmed with silverfish.

He straightened up, and as he turned away from the codex, his eyes were lusterless once more.

"A life of the Prophet," he said. "Nothing about Sicily. Merely a life of the Prophet. One of many."

Don Giuseppe turned a radiant face towards Monsignor Airoldi. "His Excellency says it is a precious codex, There is no other like it, he says, not even in his own country. It is an account of the Arab conquest of Sicily, and deals with the history of their rule here."

Monsignor Airoldi purpled with happiness; he was so moved that he stammered. "Inquire of His…" he said. "I mean, ask him whether in form it is like the *Cambridge Chronicle* or – oh, like *De rebus siculis*."

The Chaplain was not a man to be discouraged by any such vague question; indeed, he was prepared to cope with a far greater challenge. He turned to His Excellency. "Monsignor is disappointed that this codex does not deal with Sicilian matters. But he wishes to know whether lives of the Prophet, like this one, may be found at Cambridge or elsewhere in Europe."

"In our libraries we have many. I do not know whether there are any at Cambridge or in other cities in Europe... I do regret that I have caused Monsignor a disappointment, but things are as they are."

Ah, no, Don Giuseppe thought, things are not as they are, and to Monsignor he said, "His Excellency is not familiar with *De rebus siculis*, naturally—"

"Naturally, of course." Monsignor felt slightly confused.

"—but he knows of the *Cambridge Chronicle*. This codex, he says, is something quite different. This is a collection of letters, reports – affairs of state, in a word." The idea of contriving the fraud had occurred to Chaplain Vella the moment Monsignor Airoldi had proposed the visit to the Monastery of San Martino; the Bishop had remembered that the library there contained an Arabic codex brought to Palermo a hundred years before by Don Martino La Farina, Librarian of the Escorial. What better opportunity could there be to ascertain the contents of the codex? An Arab visitor conversant with literature and history and an interpreter like Vella.

Abdallah Mohammed ben-Olman, Ambassador from Morocco to the Court of Naples, was in Palermo that

December of 1782 because the ship on which he was returning to Morocco had been driven onto the Sicilian coast by
a storm and smashed. Viceroy Caracciolo, who knew what
importance the government in Naples placed on maintain-
ing friendly relations with the piratical Arab world, had acted
accordingly, albeit with concealed compunction, and, immediately upon learning of the disaster, had sent sedan chairs and
carriages, under strong escort, to rescue the Ambassador,
who was stranded on the beach in the midst of his luggage.
But no sooner had the Ambassador reached the palace than
the Viceroy realized he could not possibly communicate
with him: the man knew no French, indeed he did not even
know Neapolitan. Providentially, someone suggested that
the Viceroy summon a Maltese chaplain who could be found
wandering the city streets at almost any hour, always alone,
always morose, catapulted into "happy" Palermo by who
knows what fate.

The couriers dispatched on Vella's trail searched feverishly
for him throughout the city. At the house of a niece who
extended him the grudging hospitality of food and a roof,
he was to be found only at mealtimes and at night; the rest
of the day he was abroad, engaged in the dual profession of
chaplain of the Order of Malta and numerist. The second
activity enabled him to supplement the necessities supplied
by the first. He did not fare too badly, but he was not yet in
a position to dispense with his niece's hospitality – a most
trying hospitality, what with a half dozen children spawned
surely from the mouth of Hell, and a head of household,

husband of that niece and father of those children, who was a ne'er-do-well and a drunkard.

One of the couriers found him, finally. He was in the shop of a butcher on the Via Albergaria and was engaged in unriddling a rather confused dream for the man. For the Chaplain was not so much a numerist as an interpreter of dreams. From the dreams people told him he selected whatever elements could be arranged in a more or less coherent story, and the images that emerged most prominently he then translated into numbers. It was no easy task to reduce to five numbers the dreams of the people in Albergaria and Capo, the two sections of the city to which he confined his activity. Like the tales in the "Lives of the Paladins of France," their dreams were endless; they dissolved into a chaos of images and meandered down a thousand and one obscure byways. In the dream that the butcher was relating to him when the courier arrived, there was a pig that laughed, no less, and, to boot, the Viceroy, a neighbor woman, a meal of couscous, and and and... These were the chief elements the Chaplain had managed to extract from the stupendous dream.

He listened to the courier's message, and it struck him as a good omen that the Viceroy's summons should reach him as he was about to assign a number to the viceroy the butcher had dreamed about.

To the courier he said, "I am coming at once," and he asked the butcher, "In your dream, did the Viceroy appear in a public or private aspect?"

"What?" said the butcher.

"I said, was he with company, in a procession, or alone?"

"The way I dreamed him, it was face to face, just the two of us."

"Viceroy eleven...couscous thirty-one...four for the pig..."

"But the pig was laughing," the butcher pointed out.

"He was laughing hard."

"Did you see him laugh, or did you only hear him?"

"Now that I come to think of it, it seems to me that when he began to laugh I stopped seeing him."

"Then add seventy-seven...and forty-five for the neighbor woman."

He signaled to the courier and moved toward the door.

"Father!" the butcher shouted. "You've forgotten about – the rest of that last part!"

"If you really want to include that," the Chaplain said, and he flushed, "then make it eighty. But there can be only five numbers. Drop either the eighty or the seventy-seven."

"Not the eighty, for sure," the butcher said.

The Chaplain went out, silently consigning the fellow to the Devil.

He found the Viceroy in a state of agitation. He had no time even to bow before Caracciolo propelled the Moroccan Ambassador virtually into his arms.

"Don't tell me you don't know Arabic" – the Viceroy's pleasantry was edged – "or I'll pack you off to the Vicaría."

"A little, yes, I know a little Arabic," Don Giuseppe said.

"Good. Then show this fellow around, give him anything he asks for, satisfy every wish, every whim – prostitutes, princesses, whatever he wants."

"Excellency!" Don Giuseppe protested, pointing to the Jerusalem cross on his chest.

"Take it off, go to the stews yourself. It would be no novelty, I warrant," the Viceroy answered, with a malicious smile.

The Ambassador, henceforth chained to Vella like a blind man to his guide, had not asked to go to bordellos, luckily, for all that he did allow his slow, rheumy glance to slip like flowing honey down the ladies' low décolletages. Instead, he had asked to see everything Arabic that was to be found in Palermo. This being the stipulation, the mood of each day depended on the extent to which Don Giuseppe could satisfy it; some days he scored well and some days he missed. Fortunately, Monsignor Airoldi had intervened and, with his passion for Sicilian history and all things Arabic, had become the Ambassador's self-appointed guide while Don Giuseppe continued to act as interpreter. In this way, Monsignor had made a duty that was already lucrative for Don Giuseppe agreeable as well; he spent delightful evenings in the company of beautiful women, enchanted evenings of warm lights, silks, mirrors, beguiling music, delicate foods and wines, and illustrious company.

The realization that all this could not last beyond the departure of Abdallah Mohammed ben-Olman began to gnaw at the heart of Don Giuseppe Vella. The prospect of going back to the struggle to make ends meet on a miserly benefice and the uncertain proceeds from doling out numbers seemed to him a bitter and despairful fate.

And so, from fear of losing pleasures he had scarcely yet

savored, from innate avarice, and from an obscure scorn for his fellow creatures, Giuseppe Vella seized the opportunity that fate offered him, and with sober, lucid daring became the protagonist of a vast fraud.

Chapter II

O n the 12th of January, 1783, Abdallah Mohammed ben-
Olman departed. As the felucca set sail, his frame
of mind was very like that of his erstwhile companion
and interpreter – one of liberation and joy. It is true that
the Ambassador had been a virtual deaf-mute, but Don
Giuseppe had passed some uneasy moments. His heart, as
the saying goes, had been in his mouth for fear that a gesture
of impatience, an eloquent shrug of disappointment, might
betray to Monsignor Airoldi and the others the fact that the
interpreter was by no means so sure of his Arabic.

"Good riddance to you and to your Devil," Don Giuseppe
murmured, as the felucca melted into the coppery hot hor-
izon. And suddenly he discovered that he had forgotten, or had
never known, the name of the Ambassador. For the purposes
of his proposed fraud, he rebaptized him Mohammed ben-
Osman Mahgia, and forthwith tested Monsignor's reaction:
"Our dear Mohammed ben-Osman Mahgia," he said.

"A dear friend, indeed," Monsignor Airoldi said, "and what a
pity that he wished to leave us so soon. His counsel would have
been precious to you in the work you will be undertaking."

"We will remain in touch by letter."

"But you know how it is – to have the eye of such a man present, available … You would have brought the work forward together with more speed, with greater assurance … If Sicily were a kingdom in fact as it is in name, we could have had the ambassadorship to Palermo offered to – what is his name?"

"Mohammed ben-Osman Mahgia."

"Ah, yes … But you will do very well without him, I am sure … Remember how eager, how warm my own concern in this is. Centuries of history and of civilization exhumed from the shadows and brought forth into the light of knowledge … Oh, it is a great work, my friend, a peerless work, to which your name will be forever bound, and even my own most modest one—"

"Oh, Excellency," Don Giuseppe demurred.

"Yes, yes, the merit will be principally yours. I am – what shall I say – I am only your impresario … And, by the way, I am aware of your circumstances – your niece's house, the noisy section of town, the uncomfortable quarters. My secretary is busy looking for a house suitable for you and your work, something decent, quiet …"

"I am deeply grateful to Your Excellency."

"And I will see to it that you do not lack other signs of my benevolence – my interested benevolence, mind you, my interested benevolence," he emphasized, smiling, and extended his hand for the Chaplain to kiss. Puffing and groaning slightly from the effort, he stepped up into his gilded sedan chair. The footman closed the door; from behind the glass,

Monsignor gestured his farewell and blessing. Don Giuseppe, his hand on the Jerusalem cross on his chest, stood frozen in a deep bow that enabled him to restrain a rush of turbulent joy over a gamble risked and won.

Sunk in his own thoughts, he walked home through the crowded Kalsa quarter; women pointed to him, children ran shouting behind him – "That's the priest who was with the Turk" – "The Turk's priest" – for as the Moroccan's companion, he had become a well-known figure. Don Giuseppe did not even hear them. Tall and vigorous of frame, slow and solemn in carriage, the great cross of Jerusalem lying on his chest, he strode through that human dust, his olive-complexioned face grave and his eyes abstracted. His mind was busy juggling dates and names: like dice, they rolled in the Hegira, down the corridors of the Christian Era, and through the obscure, immutable centuries of the human dust of Kalsa; now they rolled together to form a figure or a human destiny, now they bounced noisily along blind passages of the past. The historians Fazello, Inveges, Caruso, the *Cambridge Chronicle* – all elements of his gamble, the dice of his game. "All I need is a method," he told himself, "and attention, close attention." And yet he could not fend off a feeling that the mysterious wing of piety would brush against his calculated fraud, and that human pain would be born from the dust of Kalsa.

Chapter III

"You, Excellency," the Marquis di Geraci said, "have had the good fortune to find the Arabic codices. But I ask myself this: Where will scholars be able to turn when the day comes for them to write the history of the Holy Inquisition in Sicily?"

"They will surely find documents that have been preserved in other offices, in other archives," Monsignor Airoldi said in slight embarrassment. "And then there are chronicles and diaries."

"Excellency, you yourself have shown me that these are not the same. To have put the official records of the Holy Office in Sicily to the torch means an enormous, an irreparable loss! And the time – think of the time it will take to trace other documents that have been scattered here and there and everywhere, and to reassemble and collate them... As for diaries! A man hears some nonsense or other that is making the rounds and sets it down in his diary. Like the Marquis di Villabianca – he collects gossip! His diary will be a laughingstock a hundred years from now."

"But my dear Marquis, what can you do about it? The

matter is finished and done with now. Our Viceroy saw fit to indulge in this caprice."

"If Your Excellency chooses to consider it a caprice, then it is the caprice of a pettifogger!"

"Sh-h-h," Monsignor put his finger to his lips and crossed himself.

"To the Devil – forgive me, Excellency – I say to the Devil with him and his friends and his henchmen. I call bread bread and wine wine, and what Your Excellency calls caprice I call crime. To burn the archives of the Holy Inquisition! That is burning three centuries as if they were nothing! But it takes more than fire to burn three hundred years. A patrimony, a treasure that belongs to all men, and to us, most particularly to us of the nobility!"

"*Deus, judica causam tuam,*" the lawyer Di Blasi said ironically. "The motto of the Inquisition, sir." As everyone knew, the Viceroy had ordered it chiseled off the façade of the Palazzo Steri.

The Marquis scowled at the young man. "Furthermore," he continued, with greater heat, "I ask myself how the Archbishop could have let himself be dragged into actually witnessing such a sacrilege."

"It was no sacrilege. The Marquis Caracciolo wanted to give everyone an unmistakable message, a clear warning that times are about to change. That one must deal with a certain phase of the past as one deals with plague-infected clothing – burn it," Di Blasi said.

"About the participation of His Eminence, what do you

want me to say? As our young lawyer friend so rightly points out, the times are changing," Monsignor Airoldi said.

"Some fellow by the name of D'Alembert," the Prince di Cattolica interrupted, "has had a letter that our pettifogger wrote him about all this published in the *Mercure de France*. You would die laughing to read it, that's how ridiculous it is. He says, can you imagine, that he wept when the Administrative Secretary publicly read out the decree ordering the archives to be destroyed ... Did any of you see him weep?"

"I was not present," the Marquis said disdainfully.

"I was there," Di Blasi said, "and I assure you that the Viceroy was really moved. As was I."

"I'll arrange to borrow the *Mercure de France*," the Prince di Cattolica said, glancing scornfully at Di Blasi and turning to the Marquis di Geraci, "and I'll have you read it. It's laughable, I tell you, laughable." He walked off laughing, but abruptly turned back and grasped the Marquis by the arm. "May I have a word with you?"

The Marquis glanced around as if seeking help, and his cheeks puffed in impatience, but he followed.

"The Marquis is viperous on the subject of the Viceroy," Monsignor Airoldi explained to Don Giuseppe Vella, who was standing at his side. "Just imagine, it's been hinted to him that he should no longer use certain titles – First Count of Italy, First Gentleman of the Two Sicilies, Prince of the Holy Roman Empire. How can a man possibly go on living without those titles?"

This flash of malice roused Giovanni Meli, who had

appeared to be half asleep in an armchair. "And what about the Prince, too, poor fellow!" His face drooped compassionately, as if he truly shared in the Prince di Cattolica's dilemma. "He wangles Naples into granting him an extension of six months to settle with his creditors, but no such thing, gentlemen. The Viceroy wishes him to pay them off at once. Ah, what times we live in!" He glanced down to shield the ironic sparkle in his eyes, and then looked up with a most candid and innocent air. "Not to mention the wretched Prince di Pietraperzia locked up in Castellammare for a mere nothing, for less than nothing, really. He simply gave hospitality and protection to a pair of assassins. Now I ask you, whenever in this world has a nobleman ended up in jail for such a thing?"

"Unheard of! Unspeakable!" said Don Vincenzo di Pietro, who in passing had overheard the last words; he frowned with indignation.

"The nobility, the salt of the earth of Sicily," Giovanni Meli said.

Don Gaspare Palermo concurred : "Well said, well said!"

"And our privileges, hand in hand with the freedom of Sicily," Don Vincenzo went on.

"What freedom?" Di Blasi asked.

"Not the freedom you mean, most certainly not," Don Gaspare replied drily.

"Equality!" Don Vincenzo cried banteringly, and then, changing his voice, he mimicked: "'Inequality among men is repugnant to the sufficient mind.' Sufficient mind, indeed! Fool's talk."

Di Blasi appeared unperturbed, but the reference to an article of his published five years earlier wounded him, partly because the speaker's manner and tone had been so uncivilly scornful and also because he himself no longer held a very high opinion of the essay; he felt now that he had made a mistake to publish it; it was approximate, inadequate – childish, in a word.

"Very likely you find Don Antonino Pepi's essay on the natural inequality of man more convincing," he said, with light irony.

"If Don Antonino Pepi has written that men are not equal, then I agree with him … But, just among ourselves, all these essays and articles, why, I would not wipe my behind with them."

"And you are right, sir!" Meli shouted. His fervor left Don Vincenzo perplexed and uncertain. But no, he told himself, somewhere in that enthusiasm lay a hidden sting, a poisoned thorn, for scribblers were all of a kind.

Fortunately, it was time to sit down – to cards, that is – and everyone swarmed toward the game rooms, where the servants had already set up the tables. Don Gaspare and Don Vincenzo went off together.

Meli, who had a taste for goading a companion into revealing his inner feelings, changed the subject. "Don Rosario Gregorio," he said, addressing Vella, "is going around saying the most outlandish things. That you don't know a word of Arabic, for example, and that you are inventing the contents of the codex of San Martino from scratch …"

Vella started, but then said coldly, "Why does he not come and say these things to me? I would persuade him how mistaken he is ... And then, too, I could benefit from his help, his learning. Instead of indulging in such slander, we could work together, we could collaborate on a task that is costing me only God knows what effort, what anxiety." These last pitiable words were wrenched from him almost tearfully.

"You see how meek he is, this chaplain of ours?" Monsignor Airoldi said to Meli. "A man of gold, patient, humble ..."

Vella arose. He had contrived to give his anger the semblance of offended virtue or resigned martyrdom.

"If Your Excellency permits, I would like a moment to refresh my mind."

"By all means, by all means," Monsignor urged him kindly.

Don Giuseppe moved toward the rooms where the others were at cards. He took pleasure in watching money flow through the game, in seeing destiny leap from a card or a number, in observing the reactions of these ladies and gentlemen. It was considered ill-mannered, actually, to observe a game without taking part in it, but for a priest, who was forbidden by his means and by propriety to play games of chance, an exception to the rule was made. Don Giuseppe passed from one table to another, pausing where the play was fiercest. One game stirred him particularly; it was called biribissi, and it paid off at sixty-four to one; it was quite illegal, of course, thereby giving the players the added pleasure of flouting the intrusive, the ever-intrusive authorities. Sometimes with the playing of a single card, a single number, an entire estate crumbled: Don Giuseppe, who did not lack imagination, saw the figures or numbers on the card dissolve and re-form as a tiny map of that estate – not idyllic, Arcadian fields, but real fields solidly bespeaking their rentals and revenues. And sometimes a gentleman-player did not have an estate left to wager; then he would stake the carriage that awaited him in the courtyard below, or a valet who was known to be particularly deft at dressing hair. There were such marked men, men fated to lose; at first, bad luck would glide like a serpent from one player to another, but then would come to coil about these men and throughout an evening nevermore abandon them.

The women played absently, without passion, hardly ever for more than ready cash – silver scudi, silver onzas, silver ducats. In Don Giuseppe's apprehension of that feminine world, silver was its quality or essence; the voices, laughter, music created an essence at once corporeal and illusory, reflected both in mirror and in echo; he responded confusedly to its fascination, stirred by desire and respect, prurience and chastity. This aroused no inner turmoil, however; his gratification came from allowing his eye to feast quietly on the scene before him.

While the eye of Don Giuseppe took its pleasure, his anger now appeased and all God's grace scattered before him in silver onzas and graceful bosoms, Monsignor Airoldi was saying to Meli and Di Blasi, "You see what he is like? Easily moved, impressionable, apprehensive…and particularly sensitive to the opinion of Gregorio, because he immensely

Vella

admires Gregorio's intelligence and learning. So he is quite unable to understand such an attitude – nor, in all truth, can I – such a mean, spiteful attitude. I am disturbed by it myself, I do admit. Out of respect for me he should be, if not silent, then at least circumspect."

"Your Excellency believes that Gregorio's suspicions are entirely unfounded?" Di Blasi asked.

"Entirely, my dear boy, entirely. I leave it for you to judge: we have to do here with a man of no culture, utterly lacking in any culture." He turned to Meli. "You know him well, so you can speak out. Do you believe that Giuseppe Vella has any knowledge of literature or history?"

"An ignoramus."

"Well, then, how can such a man fabricate out of nothing a whole historical period that I am competent, in some measure, to verify? How can such a man concoct a fraud that even Gregorio would find very difficult? … Believe me. Vella knows Arabic. And I will tell you one more thing: he knows only Arabic; in our own language he cannot so much as compose a letter."

Chapter IV

The house that Monsignor Airoldi had procured for him was spacious and full of light; one side faced toward the open countryside and another on a small walled garden where he could stroll for relaxation or take his siesta. One room in the house had become a veritable alchemist's den. Here Giuseppe Vella kept an assortment of inks; a selection of glues graduated as to color, density, and strength; sheets of a transparently thin, greenish gold leaf; whole reams of heavy antique paper; various metals; cups, matrices, and crucibles – in a word, all the tools and materials of fraud.

His first step had been to unbind the codex page by page. He had then carefully shuffled the bundle of loose leaves like a deck of playing cards. Indeed, his was a game of chance, calling for great ability and involving high stakes; accordingly, he had not neglected the final, propitiatory gesture – he had cut the pack into two neat piles. Then he had patiently, painstakingly replaced the leaves in the binding. This done, the life story of Mohammed was adequately embroiled; his connection with events like the war of Dû 'Amarra and the Battle of Ohod had been severed; the revelations of the Koran, on the day of the Battle of Ohod, had been interspersed among a listing of converts; and so forth. But this was not enough. Now came the most delicate part of the task – the total corruption of the text, the transformation of the Arabic characters into characters that he had decided to call "Siculi-Arabic," and that was nothing more than Maltese, the dialect of Malta, transcribed into the Arabic alphabet. That is, he was transforming an Arabic text into a Maltese text, but using Arabic rather than Latin characters; and at the same time he was converting a life of Mohammed in Arabic into a history of Sicily in Maltese. He did not waste much effort on the transformation phase, with the result that later Don Giuseppe Calleja, a Maltese who knew Arabic well, found himself unable to understand much of the text, and said that to him it appeared – only appeared – to be a Maltese document in Arabic characters.

Don Giuseppe then embellished the codex with light, wriggling lines like the legs of a fly, and with dots and hooks and loops, which he distributed over each page with a sure and careful hand. He then covered each page with a colorless glue and, with a dexterous spatula, he spread gold leaf over it to provide a uniform patina and thereby make the new ink indistinguishable from the old. After these linguistic and highly delicate manual labors, he plunged into the other task, which would engage his knowledge and imagination to their fullest – to create out of nothing, or almost nothing, the entire history of the Moslems in Sicily.

He would have dispensed gladly with what little of this history others had recorded or invented – very likely invented, he thought; he would have worked with more enthusiasm could he have abandoned himself freely to his imagination, to a frenzy of inventiveness. But Monsignor Airoldi was a meticulous student of everything ever written about Sicily up until his own day in Greek, Latin, and the languages of Europe. Also, there was that Rosario Gregorio, poised like a watchdog to seize and rend him to pieces. He must study, then, to equate imagination to whatever information was generally accepted; he must avoid what had befallen him in the early days of his adventure when, unfortunately, he had attributed the deeds of one personage to another – for example, assigning to Ibrahim ben-Aalbi the order to invade Sicily when it had been given instead by Ziadattallah. This particular equivocation had deeply perplexed Monsignor Airoldi, but his doubts had been soon dissipated by the prompt arrival of a medal especially struck off to endorse the reliability of the codex and the competence of its trans-lator. This medal reached Monsignor Airoldi in the form of a gift from the grateful Moroccan Ambassador, but it had cost Don Giuseppe, this being his first such effort, an immense labor to make it at home.

Another man would not have borne all this; his nerves would have been undone by the continual anxiety, the strained concentration on material that was both elusive and treacherous, not to speak of the mechanical labor as an engraver, a founder, and, in his own peculiar way, a restorer. Don Giuseppe, however, went about his work as happy as a lark. He was even getting plump; unfriendly tongues said that his skin glistened like the hide of a well-fed horse in the care of a good master. His sense of risk put him in his element, as did good food, money in his pocket, and the discreet portion of pleasure that he had finally attained as a possibility if not a fact of life.

He arose with the dawn's first light, after five or, at the most, six hours of sleep. His mind refreshed, he wrote down ten or so lines of what in the eyes of the world would be the translation of the Codex of San Martino, that is, the *Council of Sicily*; he checked them against chronological and genealogical charts that he had drawn up to prevent his lapsing into discrepancies or errors; if he still had doubts, he consulted the available texts; if even the texts could not dispel his uncertainty, he left a small blank space and with an asterisk flagged a few vague annotations at the bottom of the page so that Monsignor Airoldi could, according to his own best judgment, suggest an interpretation. Then he recopied it, garbling the passage with Oriental ambiguities and Italian ungrammaticisms. As an aid in devising the most colorful syntactical errors, he kept at his side the *Rudiments of the Italian Language*, by Abbot Pierdomenico Soresi.

Then a pause to refresh himself: hot chocolate; a slice of the soft sponge cake that the nuns of the Pietà faithfully supplied; a satisfying smoke; and a walk in the garden which, still glittering with frost, breathed a grateful freshness. At such moments, Don Giuseppe's senses, quickened by the Sisters' sponge cake – by its color and consistency rather than by its flavor – were intoxicated: the fraudulent world he was delineating surged up like a wave of light to invade, penetrate, and transform reality. Out of the elements of water and woman and fruit flowed the sweetness of being alive, and Don Giuseppe surrendered to it like any governor or emir whose existence he daily invented.

His labors allowed for no prolonged self-indulgence, however, and he returned indoors to his difficult task, his progress determining whether or not he would tranquilly enjoy the lunch that, killing two birds with one stone, he prepared over the fire in which he tempered his alloys. Then a brief respite in the garden, under the pergola, where he would drift into a light sleep. Finally, perhaps an hour dedicated, as he put it, to embellishing the codex or, now and again, to designing medals and coins.

Thus the hour of the Ave Maria arrived; the stroke of the bell almost always found him on the street, on his way to Monsignor Airoldi's palace or another rendezvous or to some evening gala.

As for the Mass that he was in duty bound to recite every morning, thanks to the onerous work he was engaged in, he had secured permission to say it before the little altar he had had set up in his house. But often it quite slipped his mind.

Chapter V

The days rolled by and sank, one after another, into that shadowy chaos from which, with patient study and sturdy fantasy, Giuseppe Vella was evoking caliphs, imams, and emirs. In the other world that Don Giuseppe now assiduously frequented, however, time was punctuated by the incursions of Caracciolo, and these "Caracciolisms," as they were termed, provoked a frenzy of scorn and anger.

The Prince di Trabia had already taken pen in hand, in the name of the entire nobility: "Each day our fervid prayers ascend to Heaven that the Hearts of Our Sovereigns may be moved to release us from an enslavement more cruel than that suffered by the Children of Israel in Babylon. The laws and decrees of the King are held in utter disrespect here! Fiat upon fiat flows from an administration more harsh than was ever that of the Divan. Who among us does not long to abandon all public responsibility and withdraw into a welcome retirement but certain mutual interests must be protected and oblige us to remain in a country that has been transformed into a maze of the direst dangers and disasters." The letter was addressed to the Marquis della Sambuca, Minister at the Court in Naples.

The reference to the Divan had blossomed spontaneously from the Prince's pen because there was so much talk about the *Council of Sicily* that Vella was translating and that Monsignor Airoldi regularly reported on in the drawing rooms of Palermo. Flotsam out of *The Arabian Nights* now speckled the mirror of fashion; Vella, seemingly so closed and morose, gave the ladies the impression that he bore within him the secret, the mysterious, erotic dimension of those nights; a sweep of their own fans unfurled scenes of extraordinary couplings and strenuous pleasures inspired by those same fabulous nights, but because the fans were imported from France and judged to be contraband, they were often sequestered and publicly burned by the executioner before the Palazzo Steri.

Not only fans, but every fashion came from France and flourished lushly in a society that was a labyrinth, if labyrinth at all, of voluptuousness and indolence, titillated only by the hazards of *biribissi* and adultery. True, Caracciolo made himself something of a nuisance. The ladies were now restrained from wearing the liliform cross, green on a field of peacock blue, that identified families of the Inquisition and, by extension, conferred civil immunity upon the wearer; thus it might befall a highborn lady who had permitted herself some caprice, some indiscretion, to be arrested like any streetwalker – as had, indeed, happened to the Princess di Serradifalco. Then there was the tax on carriages, together with the sequestration of those whose owners refused to pay – the Marchioness di Geraci, the Duke di Cesarò, to name two. And the arrest of the Duke di Sperlinga, the pretext

detriment of the church

being a murder he had committed in only heaven knows what fit of nerves. Not to mention the nine government posts, all generously remunerated, that henceforth would be filled not by noblemen but by ordinary state employees. Or the five prelatures, with their truly notable stipends, of which the Church had been relieved. Caracciolisms followed one upon the heels of another, to the detriment of the Church and her unfortunate priests: a prohibition against accepting the traditional obol for funeral services; a prohibition against begging for Masses and works of charity; prohibition of this, of that, with not a day passing that did not bring its fresh vexation and disclose the Viceroy poking his Voltairean nose into the business of religion.

On a late June afternoon, a storm of compassion for this condemned religion shook the nobles as they chatted at their club on the Piazza Marina, fanned by a cooling breeze that swept in from the sea. The Feast of Santa Rosalia was approaching, and Caracciolo had decided to economize; that is, to reduce from five to three the clays of public illumination and fireworks offered as tribute to the Saint. A decision so grave, this, that not even the few, the very few, nobles who were somehow devoted to the Viceroy, had the courage to defend him. They – Regalmici, Sorrentino, Prades, Castelnuovo – stood silent while the tempest beat about them. Only the lawyer Francesco Paolo Di Blasi held his ground, despite his being a pettifogger himself and, as he lived on an income of only a thousand onzas more or less, not entirely at home in aristocratic circles.

Baron Mortillaro, acting in the name of the Palermitan Senate, had already forwarded a petition to the King protesting the Viceroy's blasphemous decision. At Court, the petition would be supported by a sister of the Baron, who was married to a Spanish diplomat. The outcome – His Majesty's displeasure and disgrace for the Viceroy – was expected by return post.

"What's more, he supports the Jansenists!" The Prince di Pietraperzia's voice rose to a thundering finale.

"The Jansenists?" The young Duke della Verdura was appalled, although he was not sure precisely who the Jansenists were.

"Exactly, the Jansenists," the Prince confirmed.

"I believe that the Duke would like to know who the Jansenists are," Di Blasi suggested.

"Yes," the young Duke said.

"Well, the Jansenists are people who are mucking up the business of grace and so on to suit themselves...St. Augustine...In other words, a...a kind of heresy...But you," he turned, purpling, on Di Blasi, "why are you meddling in this? If the Duke wants to know who the Jansenists are, let him ask his confessor. When it comes to matters of faith, too many cooks spoil the broth, I say."

"But you sounded so horrified when you said the Viceroy protects Jansenists—"

"Yes, my dear sir, he does protect them. Any and everything that can tear religion down and destroy it, *that* he protects."

"You know for a certainty, do you, that the Jansenists can tear religion down and destroy it?"

"That's what I've been told. And if you want to know, the person who told me was—"

"Was your confessor, naturally."

"My confessor. And what he knows about doctrine would do for an army."

"Would an army know what to do with his doctrine, do you think?"

"You have a knack for getting me off the subject. What has an army to do with it? We were talking about the Feast of Santa Rosalia, if you don't mind."

"I don't mind."

"So … The Feast should last five days, and if someone wants to economize, let him economize in his own house. And if someone wants to repair the damage done by the Messina earthquake with the money of the people of Palermo – to divert funds from the Feast for such a thing – then I say this: let every man mind his own troubles, and if Messina has had a disaster, let Messina take care of it herself … Those *messinesi*! They're forever trying to fleece Palermo."

"I know for a fact that our pettifogger has taken steps to transfer the capital from Palermo to Messina," the Duke di Cesarò said.

"You hear that?" the Prince di Pietraperzia shouted at Di Blasi and Regalmici and Caracciolo's other friends. "Men of Palermo, are your bowels not stirred within you to hear such a thing?"

"The Viceroy has nothing against the city of Palermo," Regalmici said. "He simply believes that the concentration of nobility in Palermo makes for obstacles and delays in the work of the government."

"Which is another way of saying that he's got it in for us," said the Marquis di Villabianca.

"This is something you have just discovered?" Monsignor Airoldi smiled.

He was sitting a little apart from the group, with Vella, as usual, by his side. They had reviewed the day's work on the *Council of Sicily*; now, in silence, they were eating a delicious lemon ice, and Don Giuseppe, letting the sherbet slip down his throat in large spoonfuls, was visibly refreshed.

The Marquis di Villabianca drew his chair close to the pair and confided in a whisper to Monsignor, "Do you know what the Viceroy found on the desk in his study this morning? A message in big black letters that said 'Either five days or death!'"

"Not really!" the Bishop exclaimed delightedly.

"I had it in confidence from the Marquis Caldarera, who is a member of the official household. The Viceroy was furious, he says, like a maddened bull."

"The fact of the matter is simple: he wants to hurt us wherever and however he can," the Prince di Trabia said.

"But at last he's bitten off more than he can chew," Baron Mortillaro said fawningly; he was alluding to Trabia's letter to the Minister in Naples.

"Ah, this I don't know, my dear fellow, this I am not so sure of," di Trabia parried, and then, with deep feeling, even grief, "I fear they've lost their heads in Naples, too. The King most certainly cannot count on advisers of understanding and wisdom, of tested loyalty. If the new census and the new cadastre that the Marquis Caracciolo has proposed are actually approved, we will see some very odd things. We will be paying taxes on our estates in the very selfsame way that any bourgeois pays on a field that yields him a half salma of grain." The Prince held it to be a point of style, a proof of his own unshaken serenity, to refer to the Viceroy by title and name rather than to say pettifogger.

"Does it not seem logical to you," Di Blasi said, "and, more than logical, just, that the man who owns a half salma should pay taxes on his half salma and that the man who owns a thousand salmas should pay on a thousand?"

"Logical? Just? I call it monstrous! Our rights are sacro-sanct! Sacrosanct because every king, every viceroy, has sworn on his oath that we should have them... You are always busy looking into old customs; you ought to know as much... The freedom of Sicily, holy God!" He raised clasped hands to consecrate that freedom once again.

"I know all this, yes, and I also know about all the usurpa-tions of property and other abuses. But aside from whatever there may be to say pro or con privilege – about the substance, so to speak, of privilege as such – we must still recognize the fact that privilege, or what you call the freedom of Sicily, can no longer be maintained. It is one vast usurpation that encompasses others, endless other—"

The discussion would have ended who knows how if the Countess di Regalpetra, a splendid vision in her gown of light taffeta with white and cherry-red stripes, and with her point d'Angleterre lace fan opened over a nearly bare bosom, had not moved away from the group of her friends and called Di Blasi to her.

"Were you talking of very weighty matters? Forgive me. I called you because I wanted to tell you instantly instantly instantly that I have read that delicious little book you so kindly lent me...Delicious, oh yes, delicious...Of course, rather too, how shall I say, too daring..." A coquettish flick of the fan hid the bright malice of her smile and eyes. "But how do you manage to have all these delicious books? These utterly delicious little books?"

"I have big ones, too. The complete works of M. Diderot – since his *Bijoux Indiscrets* pleased you so – are at your disposal."

"You have more? Truly?...Does Monsieur always write about such things?"

"Diderot...No, not always."

"Ah, but *Les Bijoux Indiscrets* – extraordinary, really. I found myself imagining – can you guess?"

"What would happen if suddenly the jewels of your friends were to talk."

"How did you ever guess? That is exactly what I was imagining – and with pleasure, believe me, with what pleasure!"

"And this, I wager, is what you were thinking: If the jewels of a certain lady had talked in front of her future husband, she would have been spared having her disabused spouse lock her out to spend her wedding night on the balcony."

"Because there would have been no wedding!" the Countess laughed. Tears of amusement sparkled in her eyes, her fine bosom swelled, and her fluttering fan chased the rosy flush from her cheeks. "But you are extraordinary, you know. You really do know what I am thinking."

"I should like to know everything about you."

"Do try – but choose a better moment." Her voice was crisp with annoyance, for bearing down on them was the Duchess Leofanti, a lady of exasperating virtue. Greeting Di Blasi with a nod, she said in her rough masculine voice, "You've heard the dreadful news, I'm sure? That man! Now he's making mischief with the saints, with our Rosalia, our own most miraculous Rosalia... But he'll come to no good end. You'll see, this the good people of Palermo will not swallow."

Di Blasi took his leave with a little bow and rejoined the group he had left; it was rather fluid, flowing around Monsignor Airoldi, the Marquis di Villabianca, and Vella, who preferred to sit quietly in their chairs.

The conversation now concerned a service, a small service Caracciolo had done the city of Palermo: he had used funds from the suppressed Inquisition to establish several professorships at the Academy of Higher Studies, and intended to create others, among them one in Arabic. This chair was destined, naturally, for Chaplain Vella; Monsignor Airoldi was much pleased, indubitably more pleased than Vella himself, who was aiming not at an academic post but at an affluent prelacy, at an ecclesiastical benefice from among the wealthiest and most secure in the Kingdom. Nonetheless, he relished the idea of enlarging and complicating his game, of being able to act out his role in a less perilous plot by setting up a school, an entire school, devoted to the study of an Arabic tongue that he had founded, indeed virtually created. Thus, one daring feat successfully executed, the acrobat passes to another more daring, more difficult still.

Chapter VI

The festival of Santa Rosalia lasted five days in spite of Caracciolo and with great jubilation on the part of both nobles and commoners, united for once in the name of the Saint. The blasphemous tongues of certain people who guzzled regularly at the trough of that infamous Voltaire claimed the festival had been a source of humiliation, however, to Santa Cristina; it was to Cristina that the city of Palermo had offered homage and devotion before the time when a terrible plague had raged through the town and Rosalia had appeared before a soapmaker, authenticating certain bones found on Monte Pellegrino as her own, and informing him that three days later the plague would surely, albeit holily, carry him off. An anonymous chronicler relates how this last intelligence, far from causing the soapmaker to touch iron or indulge in other exorcisms, was for reasons of his own welcomed by him; the three days remaining to him he dedicated to going from house to house bearing the joyful news of the Saint's apparition and of the prophecy that concerned him. The chief physician of the city, Marco Antonio Alaimo, more conversant with pestilential than

like Greek gods –
trouble maker
capricious

with celestial matters, was quite reasonably concerned about the case as an infraction of public-health regulations. Santa Cristina, on the other hand, viewed it as a matter of disloyalty: Rosalia had taken advantage of the already evident decline of the plague to present herself – her with her virginal airs and rosy blond head – as the savior of the city. After biding her time for a century and a half, Cristina had seen in Caracciolo's maneuver a momentary greening of her hopes for revenge.

These same malicious tongues had it further that when her hopes of the Festival's being curtailed were blasted, Santa Cristina turned her hand to the business of famine, an activity of hers that was detrimental to the city of Palermo and to all Sicily and with which she never failed to busy herself whenever in a moment of absent-mindedness the protectress-in-office allowed an opportunity to come her way.

As this little anecdote made the rounds, it came to the ear of Caracciolo, who was vastly amused. The famine, on the contrary, worried him greatly, and he set to studying its causes and possible cures.

In Palermo, bread was in good supply and was protected by an official price list; as a consequence, all the hungry mouths of the Kingdom invaded the city. It was piteous to see citizens born-and-bred huddling in the city squares night and day, their eyes fairly shouting their hunger, their thin arms outstretched to beg for charity.

Charity the nobles did dispense: every Friday, to every poor man who presented himself outside the gate, a nauseated liveried servant distributed a small chunk of bread, whence the expression "Friday's loaf," which became the proverbial phrase to denote niggardly assistance or compensation. During public calamities, the nobles made exceptional donations, as they also did in the event of family bereavement, securing the paid prayers of the poor to refrigerate the soul of a departed relative on its way to the fires of Purgatory, for no Sicilian family, be it noble or plebeian, has ever questioned that Purgatory is the destination of its dead.

It may be said that Don Giuseppe Vella did not even notice the famine. He was working furiously from dawn to dusk, and he spent his evenings in gilded drawing rooms where not even the echo of famine penetrated. By now, all scholarly Europe knew of his work, and was eagerly awaiting its publication. Nonetheless a kind of dissatisfaction had begun to gnaw at him.

He was one of those men for whom to be respected, honored, and made much of is not enough; such men want to arouse fear, in some way to quicken a spasm of fear in those around them. The nobles now held him in very high regard; why should they not have also to fear him? What was to prevent ingenuity such as his from embellishing fraud with a nuance of blackmail?

The truth is that in his dissatisfaction, in his restiveness, he had at first thought to enliven the swindle and enhance his own fame with the announcement that he had discovered the books of Titus Livius in an Arabic translation – that is, the eighteen books by Livy, sixty through seventy-seven, that were lost to the world of scholarship. When he found himself unappeased by the excitement and trustful expectancy that

surrounded his current work, he postponed the fabrication
of Livy to a future date and gave himself to the study of a
project better suited to his talents, to circumstances, the
times, and history.

The idea came to him from a maneuver by Caracciolo
which had caused the nobles a certain alarm over and above
their usual irritation: the Viceroy ordered the marble busts
of Mongitore and De Napoli, two illustrious defenders of
baronial privilege, to be removed from the senatorial palace;
further, he ordered that two treatises by De Gregorio, *De
judiciis causarum feudalium* and *De concessione feudi*, be publicly
burned under the direction of the public executioner. Like
a hound dog that sniffs the scent in a puff of wind, Don
Giuseppe sprang to attention at the smell of burning paper.
Caracciolo was endeavoring to reduce the entire body of
feudal jurisprudence to ashes, to destroy a whole complex
of tenets that Sicilian civilization had elaborated with much
ingenuity and skill over the centuries to defend the barons'
privileges, a juxtaposition of historical facts artfully isolated,
defined, interpreted, out of which had come a juridical
corpus that had been unassailable until that moment. Now,
in the eyes of a reforming viceroy and a greedy monarch,
that massive body of legal opinion was coming to assume
the aspect of an imposture; Don Giuseppe, who understood a
thing or two about imposture, was beginning to understand
the workings of this one. It would not require too much to
reverse the terms, surreptitiously to deal Viceroy and Crown
the cards of a reversed fraud; surely they would willingly

accept the cards and discharge their debt by the conferral of a rich prelacy or abbacy. They – nobles and jurists – affirmed that in the Norman conquest of Sicily, King Ruggero and his barons had been rather like associates in a commercial enterprise, the King functioning somewhat like the president of a corporation; by extension, this meant that vassals owed the barons the same allegiance they owed the King, and so forth. Don Giuseppe would bring to light an Arab codex in which the affairs of Norman Sicily would be shown in a quite different light by the firsthand, disinterested testimony of the Arabs and by documents of these same Norman kings; that is, his codex would establish the fact that everything belongs to the Crown and nothing to the barons.

Don Giuseppe knew that this would not displease Monsignor Airoldi: the Bishop nourished mixed feelings for Caracciolo: he approved the Viceroy's attacks against the barons, his encouragement of education, his plans for reform, but was distressed by the disrespect for religion and its related interests that the Viceroy exhibited at every opportunity. However, Don Giuseppe proposed to talk to Monsignor on the basis of a codex already fabricated; never again would he be so imprudent as to chatter about it first, no matter how vaguely, for then the whole matter could end like Livy's eighteen books, which he was quite sure he would never bring himself to produce. He found the Romans tedious. The Arabs, on the contrary, he delighted in, and even as he labored, he relished a pristine indolence, an unpredictable fantasy that emanated from their world.

He would not speak of it, then. He would need several years – first to develop the work in Italian, then to translate it into his particular Arabic – in a word, to make it a codex with every semblance of authenticity. A revelation, that is what it would have to be. Meanwhile, fortified by this secret, by the private knowledge of the blow he was readying against them, he moved easily among those nobles who had at first intimidated him; he became a good, even a brilliant, conversationalist. Seeing him thus altered, Monsignor Airoldi was swept by waves of apprehension that were quickly stilled by Vella's steadily unaltered submissiveness and by his feigned innocence of history and antiquities.

To inform himself about Sicilian constitutionalism without arousing suspicion, as if acting from a sudden, disinterested enthusiasm, Vella had taken to frequenting the Di Blasis – young Francesco Paolo, who at the behest of the Viceroy was researching and preparing a commentary on early customs and traditions, and who had already published a study of Sicilian legislation; and the uncles Giovanni Evangelista and Salvatore, Benedictines both, and both students of Sicilian history. They used to meet in the Airoldi home and at the clubs, on the promenade of the Piazza Marina, or at the Ze Sciaveria, on the Marina di Romagnola, one of those places that are taken up by people who wish to avoid crowds and noise and so end up becoming crowded and noisy; or in the house of Francesco Paolo, which almost all the dialect poets of Palermo, Giovanni Meli first among them, regularly visited, and where the meetings almost always ended in discussions of poetry

passion, Di Blasi, honesty, clarity
Canon Gregorio – Unbearable

and dialect. These topics were of the most meager interest to Vella, but he derived a certain enjoyment from the recitation of poetry celebrating the beauty of women and from the flashing, rapier-like epigrams. Poems like those of Meli which sang of the brows, the eyes, the lips, the breasts, the tiny moles of Palermo's loveliest women gave him almost more pleasure than the sight of the ladies; the epigrams aimed at people known or unknown to him he enjoyed as the small coin of the contempt for others which encased him like a suit of armor. Only two persons escaped his scorn: one, young Di Blasi, whom he liked because he was young and so different from, so unlike himself – he recognized a generous passion, honesty, and clarity in this young man, who represented to him some remote, unrealized potential of his own life; and two, Canon Rosario Gregorio, whom he could not despise and therefore profoundly hated.

A rather unsympathetic man, Canon Gregorio; personal characteristics apart, he was physically unsympathetic: slim, but with the face of a fat man; a moist lower lip; a wart on the left cheek; sparse hair that fell over his forehead and at the back reached to his shoulders; round, unblinking eyes; and a coldness, a stillness, from which he emerged only rarely, with an incisive gesture of his short, fat hands. He exuded self-confidence, severity, discipline, and pedantry. Unbearable. Yet everyone stood in awe of him.

The one time, the only time, they had spoken, Gregorio had been particularly mordant. "I congratulate you," he had said, with an ironic smile. "They should dub you bishop *in partibus infidelium.*"

"Why?" someone asked.

"Because he has, I know, made great progress in converting the Moslems of Sicily and making them behave like Christians."

Indeed, in early passages of the codex that Monsignor Airoldi had already divulged, Don Giuseppe had not been too mindful to give his Moslems a deportment consistent with the rules and prescriptions of the Koran governing prayers, ablutions, the division of spoils, and the like. But from that moment, the Arabs in the *Council of Sicily* prayed, bathed, and divided their spoils with even excessive orthodoxy, for Monsignor Airoldi stood by, Koran in hand, to challenge any lapse of faith that might spring up in the codex like a weed; he called for a stern accounting, exactly as he would have taken one of his own confessants to task for meat eaten on Friday or a fast day unobserved. It was laughable. But this Gregorio was a hair shirt. He had actually set to studying Arabic by himself. Purely for the pleasure of unmasking Don Giuseppe. "Why? What is it to you?" the Chaplain asked him silently. "Am I taking bread from your mouth? Meet me squarely, talk to me privately and plainly. Say to me, 'You are playing tricks that will reap a pretty penny, and I want a share.'... And I will say to you, 'Very well, let us play together, divide half and half!'... But no, not you. You, sir, do not want to live and let live. You are a cur, a mangy, pest-ridden, slavering cur."

Chapter VII

All Palermo, from the fisherman in the Kalsa to the Prince di Trabia, was muttering over the scandal, the indignity, the outrage of the Marquis Caracciolo's having elected the singer Marina Balducci to grace his bed and table.

"Are noblewomen in such short supply?" Don Saverio Zarbo asked ironically, and his hand described a large circle that embraced the Marina promenade and the Villa Flora, which at that hour of the day was atwitter with fashionable ladies.

Every man in the group who had a wife or sister pretended not to hear or ostentatiously turned his back and walked off. Don Saverio snickered.

"A little more of such talk and you'll have a duel on your hands," Giovanni Meli said in a low voice.

"Did I mention any names? Did I call any man cuckold?"

"Worse than that. You included them all."

"And what about you? You keep putting all of them into your poems, don't you?"

"Well, with poetry it's different—"

"Prose or poetry, horns are horns."

"You really are old-fashioned, if I may say so. You still think that horns matter."

"You don't?"

"But we're not married, you and I," Meli said.

"Ho, that's capital!" Don Saverio laughed.

They had remained alone in a corner of the open area on the Marina where the nobles' Conversation Club met informally. Don Saverio's malicious gibes had a way of frequently turning it into a desert.

"Yes, no doubt about it. It's simply because we do not have wives of our own," Meli retorted.

"And our moralistic itch is hypocrisy at bottom, isn't it?" Don Saverio asked caustically. "If the others are cuckolds, they are cuckolds because of our sport... But perhaps you do not indulge in sport?"

"Not exactly in what you mean by sport."

"There are no two ways of meaning it. Either you get a woman into bed or you do not look at her. If I had to believe that the lips you are always praising in your poems were not lips that you also suck, that you don't squeeze this breast or that breast as you please – Well, let me tell you, you're a poor sort of man."

Meli sighed.

"No, no, I'm not asking for confidences," Don Saverio continued. "If I can believe that you have sound teeth and a good appetite, and can take advantage of the flesh and fruit Providence provides, that's enough. To believe that is enough for me to admire you as a poet and respect you as a man."

"Your notion of a poet smacks slightly of a grocer."

"To tell you the truth, my notion of a poet is quite different, but knowing you—" He burst out laughing, and Meli laughed too.

"I'm joking," Don Saverio said.

"I know," Meli said, who knew quite well that he was not.

The evening, all roseate and gold, began to cast off gentle veils of sea air. From the bandstand the musicians gave voice to the mood of the hour.

"Ah, yes, passion, passion, passion!" Don Saverio said banteringly; he did not realize that the word had come to him spontaneously and that only after turning it over in his mind had he voiced it ironically. "Passion we have with us always, do we not? Prostitutes are passionate, and so are cuckolds, the police, the public hangman, the Marquis di Santa Croce, the bandits in our mountains, and let's not forget our peasants – they've so much passion it runs out of their noses – and shepherds and fishermen, riffraff of every—"

"And you?"

"What do you mean, 'you'?" Don Saverio was outraged. "You what? You are asking me whether I am a man of passion? I am not. I have not a crumb, not an atom of passion in me...Passion! A business for beggars," and as Don Giuseppe Vella was passing by just then, Don Saverio accosted him brusquely: "What about you, Abbot Vella, are you a passionate man?"

Don Giuseppe started with surprise, and came up to the two men's table. "I am not an abbot," he said.

"No, but you will be, my friend, you will be," Don Saverio said.

"Thank you...I was hoping to find Monsignor Airoldi."

"He hasn't come yet," Don Saverio said, "but you'll find him turning up any moment. Sit down with us in the meantime. We were talking about passion, human passion. What are your ideas about that?"

"I would not know," said Don Giuseppe.

"Well, what about you, are you a passionate man? Do you feel anything inside you that resembles the passion our Abbot Meli here plays with in his fashionable poems?"

"I am no abbot either," Meli said.

"You're doing your very best to become one," Don Saverio said, and he turned again to Vella. "Do you feel the winds of passion sweep over you, yes or no?"

"I don't feel anything," Vella said.

"Look, let us take an example. Does a beautiful woman arouse some – let's say emotion, in you or..." The "or" hung suspended among them like a malicious sunbeam. He laughed.

"But I—" Don Giuseppe began, in confusion.

"I know. You're a priest. But you are a man too, no? I am talking to the man now. You cannot help but know what will soon be going on here on this moonless night, under these trees, among these pines of the Villa Flora. What will all these ladies and gentlemen be doing? At the moment, they are sipping iced drinks and chattering about clothes and hair styles. But you know, don't you, what will be happening here very soon?"

"What?" Francesco Di Blasi was standing behind Don

Saverio. He had arrived in company with Baron Porcari and Don Gaetano Jannello. Don Saverio invited them to sit down.

"What will be happening here?" Di Blasi asked again.

"I was talking about what will take place presently, as soon as it is dark, here in the park of the Villa Flora."

"A kiss for you, a kiss for me, a kiss for whoever you may be," Baron Porcari said.

"Much worse than that," said Jannello.

Meli corrected him, "Much better."

"I'll tell you something that happened to me three nights ago," Don Saverio said. "I was passing by the Villa on my way – well, I was going about my own business, and whom do I see – I have excellent sight, you know – whom do I see? Well, after all, better not name names. I see a beautiful lady. She is standing among the boxwood, and she is leaning over a pile of fresh cuttings as if looking for something she'd dropped. I stop. 'Have you lost something?' I ask. And she answers, cool as you please, 'Thank you, I've found it.' So I go on. But you know how that kind of thing is. After a few steps, I turn around. The lady hasn't moved, and right behind her is the Duke – I'm not mentioning his name either, because then you could identify the lady too easily."

Everyone but Don Giuseppe laughed. His attention was wandering, free and observant and amused, under the trees of the Flora. When his imagination was quickened by some scrap of conversation or anecdote or image, it took wing and he could no longer follow the talk going on around him; the others believed that he retreated voluntarily, out of modesty, and now Don Saverio said, "We must stop talking about such things. Abbot Vella finds them distasteful. Let's go back to where we started – passion, we were talking about passion," and he slapped his knee.

"What? – Oh, yes."

"Are you a passionate man?"

"Now that I think about it, I believe I am," Don Giuseppe said.

"I'm disappointed in you," Don Saverio said.

"Why?" Di Blasi interrupted. "Aside from the fact that all men are—"

"All men! That's what I cannot abide!" Don Saverio exploded.

"What difference is there between you and them?" Di Blasi gestured toward some fishermen who were mending their nets, holding them with outspread toes.

"You don't see the difference yourself?"

"No, I do not. I see equality. Only here are we, well dressed, well groomed, enjoying the cool, while they work."

"And you call that nothing?"

"Nothing at all. Unless you want to relate it to justice: then I agree that between them and us there are grave and shameful differences. Shameful for us, I mean ... But thinking of them simply as men and of ourselves as men, then I see no difference. They are men like you and like me. Eh, will those dreadful words 'yours' and 'mine' never disappear!"

"What would I be without the 'mine'?"

"A man. Isn't that enough for you?"

"But I am the more a man with my acres and my houses – as are you with an income you receive from your father and mother."

"We are the more men in the sense that, thanks to some wealth, we sit here discussing the fact of our being men and talking about the books we have read and enjoying beauty. But if you consider that our 'more' is paid for by others, we are actually 'less'—"

"This conversation is becoming a trifle complicated," Don Saverio interrupted, and to change the subject he said, "I can grant you that there is no difference between me and those fishermen, but don't tell me there is no difference between me and that man." He pointed to Don Giuseppe Vassallo, who was strolling by, his young wife on his arm; the picture they presented suggested a crab clinging to a branch of bright coral.

"He's got a beautiful wife, all the same," Jannello said.

"Through no merit of his... Poor thing, she hadn't a scrap of dowry, while that old frog is rich, rich," Meli said; Meli was well informed about everything.

"Poor but pure. I've yet to hear it said – and this is after four years of marriage, mind you – that she has decided to cuckold him," Baron Porcari said.

"How could she? Don't you see there's nothing there to cuckold?" Meli asked.

"Is there no end to this kind of talk?" Don Saverio said. "I was discussing with our Abbot Vella... What were we discussing, Abbot?"

"Passion."

"Passion... And you, if I am not mistaken, had said that you are a passionate man?"

"I think so."

"You're not sure?"

"I am not sure what you mean by the word. If you are referring to something fashionable, to a combination of things that, taken together, create a vogue – the man who affects passion because it is the stylish thing to do and becomes the cynosure of all the ladies or, in another way, one of Meli's shepherds – then I say I most definitely am not. But if by passion you mean a sense of human equality, of which the present fashion is an unknowing fruit, then I can say to you that I do in some manner share in that."

"What, what?" Don Saverio exclaimed, obtusely surprised. Indeed, Don Giuseppe was a bit surprised himself by the quick intelligence of his reply, and to find his mind assenting to an idea in which not his destiny and his happiness but the destiny and happiness of all men were mirrored. Honed by a radical contempt, his mind was ordinarily quite alien to any such concern. He felt a sudden unease, a surge of complication and conflict. "Watch your step," he said to himself; he did not mean in speech, for at the moment one could express any idea in Palermo freely and without risk; he meant in thought. "Thoughts that attract ideas are like tumors. They grow inside you, blind you, strangle you."

"You are talking like a closed book." Meli was stung by the reference to his shepherds.

"Not at all," Di Blasi said. "Don Giuseppe expressed his opinion in a remarkably lucid way. Because below the surface of fashionable pose you find real passion, passion for equality, for revolution—"

"What revolution? You smell revolution in the air?" Meli raised his head and sniffed like a dog.

"You haven't got the nose for it," Jannello said.

"But I smell it," Don Saverio said. "What's more, I see it. I can see an incensed populace accompanying the Marquis Caracciolo to the port with whistles and grimaces and showers of garbage…The very same thing that happened to Viceroy Fogliani, the very same."

"I don't deny that such a thing may happen: our common-ers are accustomed to lick the hand that whips them and bite the hand that tries to help them. It could happen. Although the Marquis Caracciolo is a different kind of man; he is no Fogliani, and his authority would be flaunted over his dead body. But that would not be revolution; it would be just the opposite," Di Blasi said.

"From my point of view, that would be revolution," Don Saverio said. "Even though, as you know, I like Caracciolo as a man."

"He is an extraordinary man," said Baron Porcari.

"Even if the Marquis Caracciolo were not the man he is," said Di Blasi, with mounting fervor, "every time I am near him, every time he speaks to me, I feel – moved, that's it, moved. I say to myself, 'This man has spoken with Voltaire, with Diderot, with D'Alembert.'…By the way, Diderot died, did you know? On the thirty-first of last month."

Don Saverio rose. "My condolences to the Viceroy," he said.

Chapter VIII

T he *Council of Sicily* was already finished: with great
skill and art, the Arabic Codex of San Martino had
been entirely corrupted; the Italian translation was ready,
although a final revision was still needed to resolve numerous
incongruities and equivocations. This, however, would be the
task of Monsignor Airoldi, who by this time had also been put
on his mettle by Gregorio and those who sided with Gregorio
or simply followed the work's progress as amused onlookers.

Don Giuseppe was now entirely dedicated to the fabrication
of the *Council of Egypt*; like a small tradesman who leaves his
shop to venture on broader winds of chance, he had had
Giuseppe Cammilleri , a monk and a trusted friend, come on
from Malta to help him with the physical labor. Cammilleri
was a man of the same stuff as himself, but niggardly and
slow of mind, with primitive, urgent appetites. In the matter
of keeping a secret, he was a tomb; it was necessary, however,
to deposit in that tomb the obol that the ancients used to
place in the tombs of their dear departed ones; and as the
money Don Giuseppe gave him disappeared, never to be seen
again, one might have supposed that it also was destined to

be an antiquarian or, in today's parlance, an archaeological discovery. He's burying the money in the kitchen garden, Don Giuseppe thought, for from time to time he took the precaution of inspecting the monk's effects, and he never found any trace of money; nor was there any sign or hint that the man might be spending it; for one thing, he never went out of the house. Actually, he was burying his silver in the pocket of a streetwalker who came to visit him between the Ave and two in the morning, when the master of the house was out: a generous fee in the monk's view, a most miserly one in the view of the lady. Thus it happened that under Don Giuseppe Vella's roof, in the house where his Bishop had kindly lodged him, her every visit was marked by an altercation in which certain physical characteristics, members, and vices were called by their crudest names.

Luckily Don Giuseppe suspected nothing of all this, for it would have been a worry and a trial to him: he could not have dispatched the monk back to Malta now that the man was the guardian of a dangerous secret, nor could he have countenanced the continuance of such a shameful performance. In any event, the house was out of the way and, when the first shadows of evening fell, was immersed in almost frightening solitude.

Oblivious of the gross passion the monk was comfortably indulging behind his back, Don Giuseppe enjoyed the man's company and his help, especially his company, after years of solitude – a solitude like that of an artist who might find himself alone on a desert island laboring on a creation that no

alito – breath

other man would ever see. Don Giuseppe was aware that his work, his real work, had elements of imagination and artistry; when, in a few centuries or, in any event, after his death, the historical fraud would be discovered, the romance he had created would still remain, the extraordinary romance of the Moslems of Sicily; posterity would enshrine his name with the golden aureole of a Fénelon or a Lesage, far different from the ominous glory surrounding the name of Giuseppe Balsamo, a Palermitan known throughout Europe as Count Alessandro di Cagliostro. His artist's despair fused with the vanity common to all men who stand beyond the pale: he needed someone, a witness, an accomplice, who in the course of the day's toil might admire in him the original creator of a literary work and the no less original and daring impostor.

The monk was not the ideal man for the purpose: he paid the sum total of his anxious admiration to the imposture, but he was unable truly to appreciate the literary work; he could do no better than limp along in the role of the marveling observer that Don Giuseppe had assigned him. He was, nevertheless, an *alito*, as Sicilians say, a breath of life, a human presence that serves to soften loneliness and despair, a light rustling of air in a burning drought. In the mechanical work, the copying and the coinage, his assistance was invaluable: he was patient, attentive, meticulous.

During the hours of work, both men were silent; they seemed deaf-mutes. But at table and while resting in the garden, they grew loquacious as they reminisced about Malta, their childhood, and their families and friends, of whom the monk had the fresher memories and more recent news. Or they reviewed their life, what it had been, how it was changing, and also touched on things of this world of which the monk was almost entirely ignorant. When it came to worldly things, he positively seemed to be a character out of the *Fioretti*; also, with regard to women, of whom he had a concealed, unconfessed, but most practical knowledge, the more deeply he became mired down in that subject, the more he floundered among vague, half-fearful fantasy and the desire and emotion that Don Giuseppe Vella relished more slyly.

"Don't you believe, really, that the Devil made them?" the monk asked.

"Why, no." Don Giuseppe smiled. "They are also God's handiwork. What merit would there be, otherwise, in our abstaining from women? To abstain from works of the Devil is easy; the difficult thing is to abstain from what God Himself has made and asks us, out of love for Him, not to touch."

"You may be right," the monk said. "No doubt you are right, you have dogma at your fingertips, but I don't see much sense in any of it. It strikes me like denying praise to God for one whole part of His creation—"

"We praise God for every part of His creation, woman included. We praise woman for her beauty, her harmony, and we exalt her as a mother. But we also make her the object of our renunciation, our sacrifice, in order to be only priests of God, entirely and exclusively His ministers."

"But can you do that? I don't mean can you do without women, but are you able not to think about them, not to dream about them, not to draw them up over you in a dream like a quilt of pleasure?..."

"That I cannot," Don Giuseppe said, closing his eyes.

And the monk was comforted. And because he had a slack memory and was subject to recurring bouts of repentance and remorse, he often brought the subject up again. In the darkness of his mind and heart, shards of superstition littered his faith; Don Giuseppe knew this very well, and therefore found the words best calculated to reassure him. Sometimes the monk even felt pangs of guilt over his work as amanuensis and foundryman.

"Am I not doing something wrong?" he would ask.

"And I?" Don Giuseppe would retort.

"Well, you too," the monk would reply timidly, not daring to raise his eyes.

At that point, Don Giuseppe would explain to him at length how the work of the historian is all deception, all fraud; how there was more merit in inventing history than in transcribing it from old maps and tablets and ancient tombs; how, therefore, in all honesty, their efforts deserved an immensely larger compensation than the work of a real historian, a historiographer who enjoyed the benefits of salary and status. "It's all fraud. History does not exist. Perhaps you think the generations of leaves that have dropped from that tree autumn after autumn still exist? The tree exists; its new leaves exist; but these leaves will also fall; in time, the tree itself will disappear – in smoke, in ashes. A history of those leaves? A history of that tree? Nonsense! If every leaf were to write its history, if the tree were to write its history, then we would say, 'Ah yes, this is history.'... Your grandfather, did he write his history? Or your father? Or mine? Or our great-grandfathers or our great-great-grandfathers? They went down into the earth to rot, no more and no less, like the leaves, and they left no history of themselves... The tree is still there, yes, and we are its new leaves. And we will fall, too... The tree that will remain, if it does remain, can also be sawed down, limb by limb: kings, viceroys, popes, generals, the great ones, that is... What we are making, you and I, is a little fire, a little smoke with these limbs, in order to beguile people, whole nations – every living human being... History! What about my father? What about your father? And the rumbling of their empty bellies, the voice of their hunger? Do you believe this will be heard in history? That there will be a historian with an ear keen enough to hear?" Don Giuseppe spoke with the vehemence of a preacher, and the monk felt mortified and ill at ease. Then the preacher gave way to the impostor, the accomplice. "But perhaps the fact of being well off, as you are here, pricks your conscience? If that is so, you have only to tell me. I will pay your fare back to Malta, and that will be the end of it." And for the monk this was, all told, the most persuasive argument.

Chapter IX

"See?...So..." the Countess said.

Out of the corner of her eye, she could see herself in the tall mirror; before her on the writing desk she could also see, reduced to a vivid miniature and set in the lid of a snuffbox, the painting by François Boucher that the Casanovites claim is a portrait of Mlle O'Murphy.

Tableaux were then in vogue. In the charming little paneled pavilion where, pleading a headache to her husband, the Countess loved to retire for an intimate rendezvous, she was now creating a remarkable tableau – a perfect copy of the Boucher painting, the tenuous light helping to equate her years to the youth of Mlle O'Murphy. She used only two elements: the *dormeuse* and her own nakedness. One could not have wished for a more glowing tableau, a more faithful imitation.

Di Blasi walked over to study the miniature more closely, then came back and looked down at the living copy. He bent to kiss its throat, its shoulders; his hand ran lightly over the smooth, warm body, pausing at every soft articulation, every curve, as if molding some rare and yielding material.

"Perfect," he said.

"This isn't in the painting," she protested, but she turned to him; her lips were parted and her breasts were full, fuller and heavier certainly than those of Mlle O'Murphy. Then together again on the *dormeuse*. Re-emerging into the red and gold light, she asked, "The artist, what is the artist's name?"

"Boucher, I think, François Boucher." He stood looking down at her as she lay on her back, no longer in the graceful pose of the painting but relaxed now, sated and languid. François Boucher, he thought, *boucher*, *boucherie*, butcher. Butcher. What mysteries every language contained. For a Frenchman, the paintings of this artist, which are so luminous, so sensual, which bespeak such delight, may perhaps have a nuance, just a nuance, of butchery. I know French, and here am I thinking such a thing, although until this moment the name Boucher has always meant for me enchantment, desire...

He turned to dress. She watched him from between half-closed eyes, lazily amused; there is something ridiculous about a man getting into his clothes; too many hooks, too many buttons, and then the buckles, and then the sword.

"Do you know what I'm reading? *A Thousand and One Nights*. It's marvelous...a bit boring now and then, but marvelous...Have you read it?" the Countess said.

"No, not yet."

"I'll lend it to you. Those Moslems are extraordinary, you know. It's all a dream, they live as if they were in a dream. What a delicious city Palermo must have been when they were here—"

"But a woman like you, blond, light-skinned, blue-eyed – you'd have been no better than a slave."

"Don't say such silly things … I'd love to know more about them, about what the Arabs did in Sicily, in Palermo; what their houses were like, and their gardens and their women."

"Don Giuseppe Vella—"

"Oh, by the way, you know him, don't you? You're a good friend of his?"

"Do you want to meet him? He's an interesting man… A little, what shall I say, closed, a little mysterious… Interesting, in a word."

"Don't say such silly things. No one interests me except you… No, I meant… Well, my husband is rather concerned. He says there's something in the *Council of Sicily* about our estates; I don't know what exactly, perhaps just mention of the name, perhaps something about a census… But he is worried that in the *Council of Egypt* more may come out…"

"Some mention, for example, of the estates' having once belonged to the Crown, with the implication that your husband's title to them is based on an early usurpation?"

"I believe so. I mean, I believe that that is what is worrying my husband… You couldn't, well, speak to Vella, find out—"

"I can find out." Di Blasi smiled.

"Only find out?" She frowned prettily; it was at once a threat and a promise.

"This is a matter of historical documents, my sweet, of history. A work that demands honesty and scruple. But" – this in a tone of jesting gallantry – "I shall tell Don Giuseppe

Vella that a very lovely lady lives in fear and trembling that the *Council of Egypt* may strip her" – he caressed the naked body and bent to kiss it – "may strip her of her estates and all her revenues…"

Chapter X

D on Gioacchino Requesens stood between Monsignor
Airoldi and Don Giuseppe Vella listening to the won-
ders of the *Council of Sicily*.

"And I want to read you something that will please you,"
Monsignor said. "If I'm not mistaken, in your family you have
the title Count di Racalmuto?"

"It comes to us from the Del Carrettos," Don Gioacchino said.
"One of the Del Carretto women married into our family—"

"I must read it to you," Monsignor said. "I must read it
to you."

He rose and from the pile of notebooks on the table, after
a moment's search, selected one. He returned to his chair and
sat down, smiling with the satisfaction of someone about to
provide a pleasant surprise.

"Now, I want to read you... here it is:

"'O my Master, most Great One, the servant of your
Honor kneels before you, he bows to touch the earth before
you, he kisses your hand, and he begs to inform you that the
Emir of Giurgenta has commanded that I should count
the population of Rahal-Almut, and that I should then write

this letter, and send it to Your Honor in Palermo. I have counted every person, and I have found there to be four hundred and forty-six men, six hundred and fifty-six women, four hundred and ninety-two male and five hundred and two female children. All these children, Moslem and Christian alike, are under their fifteenth year. Saying which, prostrate, I kiss your hands and sign myself thus: Aabd Aluhar, Governor of Rahal-Almut, by the Grace of God, servant of Emir Elihir of Sicily.'

"And then there's the date, see? 'This twenty-fourth day of Muharram, in the Year of the Prophet 385.' That would be January 24, 998. What do you say to that, eh?"

"Interesting," Don Gioacchino said coldly.

There was a moment of embarrassed silence; Monsignor was clearly taken aback by Don Gioacchino's manner.

"This is in the *Council of Sicily*?" Don Gioacchino asked then.

"In the *Council of Sicily*, yes," Monsignor replied testily.

"And in the *Council of Egypt*?" Don Gioacchino continued.

"In the *Council of Egypt*, what?" The Bishop's irritation was rising.

But Don Giuseppe had grasped the situation: Don Gioacchino was preoccupied, and rightly so, about what might come out of the *Council of Egypt* with regard to the County of Racalmuto. Indeed, Don Giuseppe Vella's new enterprise was aimed directly at such preoccupations.

"I'm saying, is there something more in the *Council of Egypt* with regard to this County or other lands that belong to my family?"

"I don't know," Monsignor said, and he turned inquiringly to Don Giuseppe.

"To this point, I myself do not know," Don Giuseppe said. "I have just started to work on it," but this he said in a tone that gave Don Gioacchino clearly to understand that in the *Council of Egypt* there might well be enough and more than enough – as Don Gioacchino phrased it mentally – to make the Requesens family "cover its arse with its hand" – in a word, they stood to lose their shirts.

"Oh, I see!" Understanding dawned on the Bishop, and he turned to Don Giuseppe to explain. "You see, our Don Gioacchino is worried that some document may turn up that concerns some of their holdings or estates and that might suggest they had been acquired by an early usurpation."

"Oh," Don Giuseppe said, all surprise, all innocence.

"I am not worried in the slightest," Don Gioacchino said. "I am sure that no shadow of suspicion will fall on the possessions of my family. But you know how it is – a *quid pro quo*—"

"No such danger," Monsignor assured him.

"Absolutely none," Don Giuseppe echoed.

"I understand," Don Gioacchino said.

He supposed that he was first among the nobles of Palermo to recognize the peril that the *Council of Egypt* and the astute man who was translating it represented – especially given the way the wind was blowing out of Naples and what with that lunatic Viceroy Caracciolo. In point of fact, many many others were already alerted; a veritable procession bearing gifts had begun to wind its way to Don Giuseppe's house:

lambs bleated in his garden; a big chicken coop was already so crowded that the fowl could scarcely move; smoked meats, cheeses, and sweets were heaped high in every corner of the house… Not to mention the tribute in the form of onzas and the invitations to dinner that snowed down upon him from every side.

lunatic Viceroy
lunático
il pazzo
matto – made, nuts, insane

Chapter XI

"The Countess Di Regalpetra is in a state," Di Blasi said to Don Giuseppe, "and it's all your fault."

"Mine? But I scarcely know who she—"

"She's afraid something will turn up in the *Council of Egypt* that will wreak havoc with her revenues, and she begged me to ask you about it."

"Do you care?"

"About the Countess, at the moment, yes. About the question of her income, somewhat less."

"I will see, and let you know. But I think she has nothing to fear." He spoke with an understanding, an even <u>conspiratorial</u>, <u>smile</u>, as if to add "thanks to your recommendation and my friendship for you."

At that instant, from Don Giuseppe's words and from his smile, Di Blasi had the impression that here was a man prepared to sacrifice a passage in the *Council of Egypt*, to tamper with a historical fact, with a historical document, for the sake of friendship. It was a fleeting impression, a tiny doubt as to Don Giuseppe's professional probity. For that <u>matter, most</u> Sicilians place <u>friendship above all else;</u>

it would not be strange if Don Giuseppe shared that attitude. Later, much later, when Di Blasi thought back, the meaning of that little episode became clearer: What Don Giuseppe was prepared to sacrifice to friendship was not historical data but potential blackmail; the fact, the human and consoling fact, still remained that such a man would place disinterested affection above fraud and blackmail, that he would renounce personal satisfaction and profit in the name of friendship.

Now, however, Di Blasi was mildly disturbed, and he was about to explain to Don Giuseppe that he had only been joking when he spoke of the anxiety of the Countess – let come what must, whether good or evil and for whomever, from the *Council of Egypt* – but at that moment, the Prince di Partanna, joyous as a dog that has found its master, came bounding toward Don Giuseppe: "My dear Abbot Vella, happy are these eyes that look upon you again! Where have you disappeared to? You haven't come to see me for a week—"

"My work," Don Giuseppe said, "my work."

"That blessed *Council of Egypt*, I know, I know…but a man must take a little rest…Do you know, I find you a bit thinner, just a trifle worn?…You must take care of yourself, my dear friend, get some rest, allow yourself a bit of vacation. Come stay at my home, with me…You know the saying, 'Better a live donkey than a dead doctor.' What do you want to do, kill yourself over the *Council of Egypt*?"

"If I had not been working, I should not be able to tell you now that I have found an illustrious ancestor of yours in the *Council of Egypt*: Benedetto Grifeo, which in Arabic is pronounced 'Krifah'; ambassador from the Court of Sicily to Cairo…"

"Really? But this is a pleasant surprise!" He took Vella's arm and drew him aside. "You deserve all my gratitude, my own and my family's."

"I merely translate what is in the codex."

"Which is to say, you are deserving of a great deal, believe me…By the way, did you receive a small *cadeau* from me?"

"Forty onzas," Don Giuseppe specified; the tone was chill.

"A mere nothing…I intend to do more, and so have the honor of sharing in your glorious, your truly glorious task, to contribute—"

"Mine is very humble work; it is your patronage that makes it not only possible but worthy—"

"Don't speak such foolishness! You—"

"May I have the honor of bidding you good evening?" The Marquis di Geraci placed one hand on the shoulder of Don Giuseppe and the other on the shoulder of the Prince; he stood between them, smiling, affectionate.

"I was just thinking of you," Don Giuseppe said. "Because, as I was remarking to the Prince, I have read in the *Council of Egypt* that an ancestor of his, one Benedetto Grifeo, was the first Norman ambassador to Cairo…And do you know who succeeded him after his death?"

"An ancestor of mine, I wager," the Marquis said.

"Just so. A Ventimiglia, which the Arabs pronounced 'Vingintimill.' For the moment, I don't know exactly whether this Ventimiglia is the same – Giovanni by name – who took as wife one Eleusa, the widow of a nephew of Count Ruggero; Sarlone was her family name. The passage is a bit involved, and I am still working on it. I will have it all straight in a few days."

"You are a great man, my dear Abbot, a great man," Ventimiglia said. (By then everyone was calling him Abbot, and so we shall begin to call him Abbot also.)

What is written is written, the Prince di Partanna was thinking, but something tells me I made a mistake to send him only forty onzas. A blood relationship with Count Ruggero cannot be worth less than a hundred. Ventimiglia was sharper than I am.

Passing by with his wife on his arm, the Duke di Villafiorita waved cordially, but his smile was directed particularly at Abbot Vella, who had provided him with an ancestor in the Norman Royal Council.

Yes, yes, they thought a world of the Abbot, these nobles did; this evening gala, held at Santa Cecilia to bid farewell to Caracciolo, who was finally leaving, seemed to turn into a gala in his honor. Abbot Vella, however, was inflexible: he accepted their *cadeaux*, he was flattered by their affability, but he stood prepared to assign important posts and grand family ties only to ancestors of those who showed themselves more generous. As for granting them titles to their estates, nothing doing: he was working for the Crown; it was from the Crown that he was expecting in recompense an abbacy or other benefice *sine cura*; just as he had already obtained a chair at the Academy and a grant of a thousand onzas to travel to

Morocco for study, a project that he was just then readying himself for. And for their part, the nobles were seemingly content with the appointments and honors that Abbot Vella was distributing among their forebears, much as they yearned to have for themselves a cross or a commendation or a ribbon from their King, from the Pope, or from any other potentate.

In reality, they were calculating that despite all the uproar over how the *Council of Egypt* would deal their baronial privileges a rude blow, some exceptions there would have to be; that an appointment as ambassador or councillor must constitute the premise to the exception. And Abbot Vella allowed them to hope in this way.

Ordinarily they all greeted him, complimented him, but this evening they did so ostentatiously to show Caracciolo, the guest of honor for the evening, how little they thought of him. The party had been arranged over great opposition and only because Grassellini, Judge of the High Civil Court and a Caracciolo man, had insisted: *Tu, Grassellini, mulus Caraccioli.*

The nobles were bidding their real farewell to the departing Viceroy with sonnets and epigrams of scathing invective, rhymed satires, anecdotes, and nicknames that pilloried Caracciolo's lack of piety, his libertine tastes, and his maladministration. One of the sonnets making the rounds had Santa Rosalia, mindful of how Caracciolo had tried to undermine her fame, raising a paean of joy to heaven; Meli recited it to a small circle of listeners, with his habitual flourishes and winks, but swore that the sonnet came from another's pen; it had been sent to him anonymously. And this was true.

The Viceroy was sitting in the center box, surrounded by the highest-ranking dignitaries of the Kingdom. He appeared to be asleep. His heavy, sagging features betrayed evident age and fatigue, but now and again an ironic smile or a sharp glance animated his face. Watching him from the parquet, Di Blasi thought that he could discern behind the fleeting expressions of boredom and irony the man's profound melancholy. Awareness of defeat, of imminent death, must be acute in such a man, the young lawyer was thinking: Sicily and the Court had inflicted public defeat on him, and his own body was surrendering to death. He had had twenty years in Paris, had hoped to stay there for whatever years of life remained to him. He was already old, yet they had sent him, at sixty-seven, as Viceroy to Palermo; from the citadel of reason to the *hic sunt leones*, to a desert where the sands of an irrational tradition bury the trail of any forward-moving spirit. But he had a vigorous mind and a character that drew energy and determination from opposition and obstacles; he had immediately launched an attack against the centuries-old edifice of Sicilian feudalism. He had had to contend with the open resistance of a nobility jealous of its privileges to the point of blindness and with the now open, now covert, opposition of the Court in Naples, where the Sicilian Marquis della Sambuca held the post of Minister for Sicilian Affairs. What he had managed to achieve under such conditions established the bases for revolution in Sicilian history. He had singled out and exposed the sore spots, the paralyzed ganglia of Sicilian life: even if he had not succeeded in healing or amputating them, he had left a clear diagnosis for those few people who were genuinely concerned and sincerely eager that in their country law should replace caprice, that a government based on order and civil justice should supplant baronial privilege and anarchy, and ecclesiastical privilege too.

He had done what lay in his power to do; at times he had perhaps exceeded his authority. And yet, Di Blasi reflected, such a man could not but feel defeated. What he left of enduring achievement was entrusted to the conscience of the future, to history: tomorrow the stroke of a pen would be enough to re-establish the privileges he had worked to demolish, to restore the injustices he had been able to correct; an adultery at Court, a royal favor, a servile intrigue, any one of them would suffice.

The dramatic performance was over and now they were waiting for the curtain to rise on the farewell pantomime.

"A farewell party?" the Prince di Pietraperzia was saying. "I'd gladly give him a farewell party – whistles and catcalls from the Royal Palace to the port!" The eight months he had spent in prison still rankled.

"Grassellini, that cuckold!" Don Francesco Spuches snorted.

"But at least he's not enjoying himself," Don Gaspare Palermo said. "Look at him, he looks like a moulting cuckoo."

"Party or no party, the important thing is, he's leaving," the Marquis di Geraci said.

"But he is going to take the post of Minister, is he not?" Abbot Vella asked innocently.

"What difference does that make? Let him be Minister in Naples. We will be right here, enjoying some peace, for a change – and with a new viceroy, a man, I tell you, who is made of the stuff of angels."

"The new viceroy is who?"

"The Prince di Caramanico, Don Francesco d'Aquino. A great gentleman—"

"And a handsome man, too," the Duchess of Villafiorita said.

"They say—" Don Gaspare hesitated – "people say that Her Majesty … people merely say, mind you … Well, that there's an attachment – nothing out of order – sympathy, good will…"

"Ah yes, so they say," the Duchess assented.

"Let's put it this way: people know it for a fact." The Marquis di Geraci, because of his titles, the very titles Caracciolo had tried to strip him of, felt close to royalty, and therefore in a position to be indiscreet even about gossip that touched the throne. "Let us say that people know it for a fact … And I tell you this, our good fortune in having Don Francesco as our Viceroy is the result of the Queen's fancy for him. Acton was anxious to be quit of a man who could have rivaled him in the Queen's affections, and a man who might have won, too."

The curtain rose. From the back of the stage, a beautiful woman came forward; she was wrapped in a green fringed mantle that seemed to be made of seaweed and maidenhair fern. She stood motionless for a moment in a stricken pose intended to suggest that she was being choked by an invisible cord of grief. Then she flung back the cape; dressed only in flesh-colored tights, she looked completely naked. As she let the cape fall, her swelling bosom heaved like the prow of a galleon mounting a wave; on it was emblazoned a riven heart and, in jagged blood-red letters, the legend *Tumulus Caraccioli*: the nymph Sicily had buried her beloved Caracciolo in her broken heart.

There was tepid applause.

"The heart of Sicily was broken by her cruel government," the Marquis di Villabianca said; this struck him as quite witty, something he should be sure to set down in his diary.

"I should be enchanted to have such a tomb," the Viceroy was saying, meanwhile, to the Judge's wife, his glance plunging down her bosom, which was no less generous than the mime's. He arose, signaling that the gala was at an end.

When he came down into the lobby, he found all the guests lined up for the final farewell. He paid a compliment to every pretty woman present and singled out several of the men with a witticism or personal greeting. He asked Meli to bear in mind that when his poetry was eventually published, he could be counted on as a subscriber. He asked Vella whether the Arabic type had arrived from Parma for the printing of the *Council of Sicily,* and at what point he stood with the translation of the *Council of Egypt.* He clasped the hand of Canon De Cosmi for a long time in his own while he spoke affectionately with him. The Canon had tears in his eyes. The word "Jansenist," loaded with scorn and revulsion, coiled among the nobles crowding around them.

Di Blasi was among the last. The Viceroy inquired after his

research on Sicilian traditions, but he seemed lost in thought as the young man was answering him. Then, in a final salute, he turned to the company and with a smile said, "How can any man be a Sicilian?"

Part Two

Most Holy and Royal Majesty,

It has been reserved for the most felicitous era of Your Reign, Sire, to witness the recovery of long-lost and precious memorials of the History of Sicily, and their translation into the common tongue, thus bringing light and knowledge to where once there had been only darkness and doubt. We long lacked any account, civil or military, of that entire period during which Sicily was subject to the Saracens; and then, through a happy occurrence, about which Your Majesty is well informed, there was found in the Library of the Royal Monastery of San Martino an Arabic Codex which, containing an accurate record of all that happened both in time of war and in time of peace, has fully acquainted us with two and more centuries of Sicilian History. But then as the era of the Conquest approached, when the valorous Normans took possession of the Kingdom, history was again cast into shadow, and in default of other authority, it was necessary to lend credence to the almost entirely suspect chronicles of a few who, writing in that period, had set down the most illustrious deeds of those Norman Princes, and the most notable facts concerning them, but who preserved almost total silence regarding the early laws that they laid upon the people, and about the political constitution, the foundations of which they established.

Having acquitted myself to the best of my modest abilities in the translation of the Martinian Codex into the vulgar tongue, and while, on his part, the most esteemed Monsignor Airoldi girded himself for the task of enriching the Codex with a wealth of annotations, I, for my part, undertook another work written in the popular tongue of Araby, proposing to translate this new Codex, which I now present to Your Majesty, and which had been sent me by that generous Mohammed ben-Osman Mahgia who, returning from Naples (where Your Majesty graciously received him as Ambassador from the Emperor of Morocco), and he sojourning here for some months, conceived such close friendship for me that, safely restored to his own country, he did offer me many evident tokens of his most liberal sympathy for me. Indeed, it is to him that I am indebted for several pages that were missing in the Martinian Codex, and for various elucidations of the history of the Arabs, and for many medallions that combine marvelously together to illustrate that manuscript, and, most of all, for this Codex, which contains all the official letters that were exchanged over a period of almost forty-five years between the Sultans of Egypt, the renowned Roberto Guiscardo, the First Count Ruggiero, and the son of that Ruggiero, who bore the same name and who later founded the Kingdom of Sicily and first assumed the Royal title.

Matters of great moment and most significant information were contained in this Codex, or so it seemed to me upon translating only a few pages of it; however, mistrusting my own judgment, I thought it well advised to submit these pages to the lofty discernment of the Prince di Caramanico, who so worthily safeguards Your Majesty's interests in Sicily; and he, recognizing the value of the work, and being a tireless Patron of letters, encouraged me to persevere in the work which has now been brought to completion, and that not without travail, albeit the time I devoted to this end has seemed to me to be most excellently compensated by the utility of the work.

It remained only for me dutifully to present to Your Majesty an accurate copy of the Arabic Text, together with my version of the same in the vernacular exactly as it came from my hand, and it is this duty which I herewith fulfill. I shall be most fortunate if Your Majesty, turning for a few moments from the precious attentions with which you guard and govern two most blessed Kingdoms, will honor my Codex with Your August perusal, and read therein how the two famous Heroes, Roberto and Ruggiero, made a treaty with the Sultan of Egypt, following a most bloody war. How then, having set their affairs in order abroad, they turned to the internal administration of their domains, and laid down the first laws for the government of the people in several well-conceived articles, all abounding in those principles most calculated to protect the domestic security of the realm and to advance the well-being of its subjects. How similarly they dedicated themselves to the introduction of new arts, the making of silk especially, causing skilled craftsmen to be brought from Egypt, and establishing them here with liberal emoluments and under their permanent protection. Also, Your Majesty will observe in this same Codex with what prudence and sagacity affairs of State were conducted by the Council that these Norman rulers established, and with what uniformity, in those early times, all decrees were directed toward encouraging the progress of the nascent nation. With what sublime discernment they joined several elements of the Frankish constitution to what the Moslems had already established in Sicily, some remains of which still survived then, whence was formed a corpus of laws truly and properly Sicilian, the which, being for the most part still in force today, can, I believe, be far better comprehended and applied in the light of the Codex.

But what makes me most hopeful that this work may be found deserving of Your August protection, O Sire, is that nowhere more than here are the Supreme rights of Royal authority fully and shiningly set forth: by way of example, in two legislative provisions that are here included, and particularly in the first of these, where all powers that were reserved to be the exclusive and unalterable dominion of the rulers of this Monarchy may be read in detail; the direct and universal patronage over all the Churches of the Kingdom and the right to appoint Bishops, are seen to be firmly vested in the Royal Person, and to have been regularly exercised without challenge; the bitter struggle over control of the Illustrious city of Benevento and many other most critical struggles of the same nature are herein described, and, further, many historical questions regarding the descendants of Ruggiero, the titles of Duke and First Count – the first assumed by Roberto Guiscardo, and the second by Ruggiero himself. All these things, O Sire, with the guidance of this Codex will from today henceforth be administered more felicitously, with greater dignity redounding to Your Royal Crown.

My remarks could be further extended, did I wish to indicate, step by step, how much else of value there is in a document that has elicited the most curious expectancy among Your Majesty's subjects and among foreigners as well: let this important task be reserved for others more competent in the matter, I wish only, if Your Majesty graciously permits, respectfully to inform you that so soon as there is no further need for me to consult it, this authentic and precious Codex will be my not unworthy gift to the Royal Library, to this end, that if and when some scholar in this field might wish to examine any passage or to compare my version with it, he may be able at any time to find it without fear that it be someday lost or fall once again, as in the past, into oblivion. Indeed, I must also add that, having with some success amassed a rather rich collection of Islamic coins and vases, which I flatter myself may, as of the moment, be unique in Europe, and which I do not even now neglect to enlarge, so soon as the editions of the two present Volumes shall be published, which for the moment engages my entire time, I shall gird myself with all diligence to open the Kufic Museum, a repository capable of providing much enlightenment to distinguished scholars in verifying the various historical periods of these two Kingdoms, the Kingdoms of Spain and of Africa, and the Empires of Asia; and that further will help them to learn at what levels the various arts were practiced in those early centuries. As to the achievement of so unusual a collection, I will freely confess the truth: it cost me much labor and effort; I had also to be content that I should be deprived of many comforts of life in order to acquire it; but how far would I have lagged behind, had it not been for the courteous assistance extended to me by my correspondents in Morocco, and here by one whose kindness equals his great learning and indefatigable study, Don Francesco Carelli, Secretary General of the Government of Sicily, whom I am proud to call a friend of mine, as he gladly is of all those who labor fruitfully in scholarship and the arts. May God favor my plans, but may He above all, for the good of these Your Majesty's realms, preserve and bless Your Majesty together with Her Majesty the Queen Consort and the Family Royal.

> Your most humble servant,
> Giuseppe Vella

Part Three

Chapter I

A cavalry squadron headed the funeral procession. Then, between two rows of halberdiers stationed on either side of the street, the Captain General of the city marched alone, his step slow, his face impassive. Behind him came the nobles, dressed, as was he, in black: some thousand individuals striving, without appreciable results, to walk in step and keep their ranks straight. Next followed an infantry battalion and the military band, its brasses sounding a lugubrious funeral march calculated to stir the very bowels of shopkeepers and the rabble. Then came: the Confraternity of the Whites, the Confraternity of Charity, and the Confraternity of Peace; from the city's convents, a swarm of abandoned children, abandoned bastards, and plain orphans; the religious orders – Capuchin, Benedictine, Dominican, Theatine; the Chapter and lesser clergy of the Cathedral; the chapel choir, lighted tapers in hand, chanting a mournful dirge; the Palace Guard; the Palace service staff, dressed in mourning livery and carrying two empty caskets, one draped in black, the other in red, both emblazoned with the D'Aquino coat of arms. A short interval, and then came the head groom of the

D'Aquino stables, on foot; on his outstretched hands, palms turned upward like a tray, he bore a sword; behind him, but on horseback, came the aide-de-camp.

Lying on a bier swathed in a silk and gold flag, Don Francesco D'Aquino, Prince di Caramanico, Viceroy of Sicily, looked like a deflated wineskin embellished with waxen heraldries (two hands, folded) and topped off by a head that seemed all nose – a carnival proboscis. He was borne aloft on the shoulders of brothers from the three noble Confraternities, and flanked by others; the Prince di Trabia, second-ranking nobleman of the Kingdom, headed the line that followed; next marched the Prefect; then the Senate and all its officers; then came more cavalry, the Swiss Regiment, and the carriages of Court and Senate. Four pure-bred horses, caparisoned in black, held firmly at the bit by their grooms, brought up the rear of the cortege. In bygone days, at the end of the ceremony the four splendid beasts would have had their throats cut; now the spectators were speculating what price they might have fetched and commiserating with their fate, unaware that, on this occasion, they would prudently be spared.

It was a warm, summer-like January day. After almost ten years, the Prince di Caramanico was taking his departure with more pomp than had attended his arrival. With Caracciolo Minister of Sicilian Affairs in Naples, his long vice-regency had commenced with Caracciolian vigor, but it had been tempered and restrained by formal correctness, and little by little had subsided into apathetic respect for the old order, the old ways. As his viceroyalty drew to an end, hope for Caramanico and for the Sicilian people was vanishing like the tail of a rat into a hole, but the Viceroy was no longer, and the Sicilian people were not yet, in a position to realize this. For the moment, nobility and populace joining a taste for pomp and splendor with genuine grief for this man who had preferred to seek a popular consensus before acting, Palermo was in mourning. And because the outside world was rumbling in revolutionary turmoil, a suspicion had spread throughout the city that the death of the Viceroy might have been the result of a worldwide ferment: he could have been poisoned, this good Prince di Caramanico, could have been poisoned thanks to that weakness of his for the French, or thanks to that weakness of the Queen's for him.

To Abbot Vella, except that a dart of sunlight was stabbing him in the neck and he, pinioned in the procession, could not escape it, the death mattered not one straw; whether the Viceroy had died of a cirrhotic liver or of poison administered by some servant was a question he left for others to fret over. He had quite different worries of his own. Before him in the procession, flat and heavy as a crow's nest, bobbed the head of Canon Gregorio, his enemy and his persecutor. Abbot Vella silently converted the conjectures and suspicions about the death of Don Francesco D'Aquino into curses on Gregorio: gravel, cancer, poison. Oh, those French! Like pines afire in the dry mid-August countryside, their revolution was flaming along the shores of the Kingdoms of Naples and Sicily, along borders of both salt and holy water. The Abbot himself viewed the Revolution as a good thing, because in

France it had sealed the lips of a certain De Guignes, who had advanced several doubts about the *Council of Sicily.*

Thanks to Gregorio, Abbot Vella now found himself riding the crest of a wave of well-being and triumph, but also in peril of sinking back into far worse conditions than he had escaped. Supporting him was Tychsen, the famous Orientalist and professor at Rostock; but his enemies had dredged up a man called Hager and had had him fetched to Palermo; they were hovering over him, flattering him, regaling him royally – all at the King's expense, no less. Tychsen, a great scholar, had pronounced Vella's skill "beyond compare" and "almost divine"; this Hager, who knew little or no Arabic (Abbot Vella could swear with a clear conscience to the fact that Hager knew less Arabic than he), presumed to sit in judgment on his work. All Palermo was on Vella's side, to such an extent that Gregorio and his friends feared, or made a great show of fearing, an attempt on Hager's life. Such a design was not entirely alien to Abbot Vella; at the moment he simply found it inopportune; moreover, the problem was rather to strike at the head – at Canon Gregorio, that is. But who could say what fresh troubles might not arise to plague him if he made such a move? What he must do was remain cool, await his adversaries' moves with a vigilant eye but with an air of indifference, unconcern, mockery. Meanwhile he was the great, the celebrated Vella: Tychsen venerated him, the Academy of Naples had elected him to membership, the Pope personally worried over his health (he had had an eye fluxion, and the Pope had written to beg him to take care of himself;

sight was particularly precious to a man who from faint and uncertain signs was restoring the memory of the past).

Meanwhile, as Hager, on authority granted him by the King, had requested that the codices be made available to him for study – and the coins and the letters from the by now renowned Ambassador from Morocco as well – Abbot Vella had swept his house clean of everything that could compromise him: the night the Viceroy lay dying was a moment in which even the police had lost their heads, and it was then that he had reported a robbery. It had been a trying night: he had had to dispatch all the material to his niece's house, her husband and the monk acting as porters; then the neighborhood had had to be aroused; then a scene of despair over the disaster that the thieves had wreaked upon his head; then in the middle of the night, he had had to rush off to the Court of Justice and thus risk the danger of really running afoul of robbers. A trying night. But such was his nature that he found a kind of consolation in the thought that the Prince di Caramanico had spent a worse one: the notion came to him suddenly as in the Church of the Capuchins the nobles were lowering the corpse into its double casket.

Chapter II

As he did every morning at dawn, he threw open the
window that looked out over the garden. It was just one
week since he had reported his robbery, and as Abbot Vella
glanced down, he saw two figures moving about under the
trellis of the grape arbor. Could real robbers have come? he
wondered; but the two had heard the window open and they
came over and called up to him. Police.

"What are you doing here?" the Abbot asked.

Judge's orders, they said. They'd spent the whole blessed
night out in the open. They were blue, numb from cold.

The Abbot went to the window that looked out over the
front gate and street: two others. "Suppose I really had been
robbed, I'd have been in a fine fix. The police turn up one
week later. And to do what? They installed the iron doors on
the Treasury of Santa Azata, after it had been robbed. That's the
law for you." But he felt a vague uneasiness, a presentiment:
he hurried to the kitchen to burn the few papers still lying
about which to a trained eye might conceivably betray some
hint of, or at least raise a suspicion about, his game.

The sun was high when the judge arrived followed by

a handful of police. It was Grassellini, Judge of the Royal Patrimony. The Abbot was surprised; he had been expecting a judge of the Criminal Court.

"When a theft is a theft," Grassellini explained, "the Criminal Court has jurisdiction; but the fact is that what was stolen from you belonged to you, I would say yes, materially, but morally it belonged to Sicily, to the Kingdom, to the Royal Patrimony. There's been a small conflict of interest between the Criminal Court and the Tribunal of the Royal Patrimony; you know how these things are. But we won, naturally... Would you agree that we were in the right?"

"What else?" the Abbot said. "Papers that serve to make history belong to the Kingdom; they are a heritage, like the Normans' palace or the tomb of King Frederick."

"That is precisely the line I took. I am glad you see it in the same light...To my colleagues in the Criminal Court, however, it appeared to have some connection with revolution and such, but then, they make no distinction between the theft of a sausage and the theft of the *Council of Egypt*... That is the name of the codex they stole from you, is it not? But I make a distinction, I make a very great distinction!" Then his tone changed, and to the police he said, "Make a thorough search. Collect every piece of paper you find, every scrap, no matter how small."

The police scattered through the house. Abbot and Judge eyed each other for a moment, each taking the measure of the other and of his game, as if they had been seated at the table, cards in hand, about to begin a round of primero.

"Merely a precaution," the Judge explained. "If the thieves were to take it into their heads to pay you another visit, it would prevent them from carrying off anything else of interest to the Royal Patrimony."

"I do not think they left anything of the sort you would be looking for, but then, of course, a thorough search by experts like your people…"

"I, too, am convinced they left nothing… Completely convinced," the Judge said. His frustration was ferocious, like that of the dog unable to pursue the hare into the brambles.

The Abbot began to speak of the theft: three masked men had broken in on his sleep so suddenly that at first he could not tell whether they belonged to a dream or to reality. He had grasped the true situation when he realized that a rifle was aimed at his mouth. But what he could not understand was, what could have moved thieves to enter his home, the humble house of a man of books?

And, in fact, all they had carried off was papers, papers that could have held no value for them.

"Possibly they are also 'men of books,'" Grassellini echoed the phrase with constabulary humor.

"You think so?" Vella started in alarm. "If it is really as you suspect, if my enemies have been capable of going to such lengths, then from now on I shall have to be mindful of my own safety, of my life even." This he delivered so persuasively that the Judge had a moment's perplexity, a fleeting doubt.

"Actually, I have arranged for your house to be guarded day and night."

"I am greatly obliged to you. For I am not well. Ever since that accursed night, I have been in such a rage that I've felt as if my head would burst. But if I know that someone is standing watch, at least I can go to bed without fear."

"But you do have that monk to keep you company, and he's so goodhearted, so devoted…" Grassellini insinuated.

"Oh, no, he left some time ago… To be more exact, I asked him to leave. He was not so goodhearted or so devoted as you think. He wronged me, betrayed me… Can you imagine that here in my house—" he blushed and stammered but yet could not contain his indignation – "he used to receive – well, I shall say no more." He had chanced to discover the monk's vice and was turning it now to his own advantage.

"He used to receive what?"

"A woman of ill repute," the Abbot whispered.

Why, you old fox, Grassellini thought. You're maneuvering yourself into a safe corner. Whatever the monk has to tell once he's caught, you will say that his story is dictated by revenge.

The police, it was clear, were lingering over their search for pure love of their art: the art of turning a house topsy-turvy, of poking into everything.

Adroitly the Abbot brought the conversation around to Marquis Simonetti, who had been a close colleague of Caracciolo and was now Minister in Naples: one could imagine his distress, the Abbot observed, at the news that the manuscript of the *Council of Egypt* had been purloined.

"That is precisely why I am taking so much trouble," Grassellini said. "I shouldn't want His Excellency to question my concern, my zeal." The tone and words veiled both hypocrisy and threat. I will sew you up in such fashion, he was actually thinking, that His Excellency will not be able to lift a finger to help you.

It was not that Grassellini had anything personal against the Abbot or against Minister Simonetti; what was at work in him at the moment was that peculiar intuition of imminent change that some civil servants have; they smell change in the air before it happens and quickly make their little jump this way or that so as to be in line with the new order (or disorder) of affairs. He had been ingenuous enough to compromise himself over Caracciolo, even to the extent of promoting his farewell party; for that the nobles had flailed him alive afterward, or at least they had tried to hinder him in his career, and had made life generally hard for him. Back then, in the days of Caracciolo, he had been a young man. By now he had had so much experience, his nose was so sharpened, that he could smell it already: the government's heavy pressure on the Sicilian barons was about to be relaxed whether Simonetti remained as Minister or not, because finally the tumultuous events abroad were arousing echoes of fear and reaction in the Kingdom. The time was coming when the King would need the barons; already one indication of this was the Court's willingness to extend the term of their debts, to facilitate payments, and even to pay off the debts. Grassellini had thrown himself into the Vella affair to redeem himself in the eyes of the Sicilian nobles; he would nail a charge of simulation on the Abbot, from which a charge of fraud would follow more easily. And if he was both tenacious and devious in carrying out his duties, he was conscientious too, after his fashion; he had no doubt that Abbot Vella's codices were frauds and his robbery also a lie. One had to proceed with tact, of course, with prudence, and he would run with the hare – Simonetti, Monsignor Airoldi, and Abbot Vella – and hunt with the hounds – the nobles.

The police brought everything they had found and piled it at his feet. The Judge ordered all papers packaged and sealed. With much ceremony and repeated admonitions to the Abbot that he take care of himself, he took his leave.

"I shall go to bed at once," Vella assured him. "I really have scarcely the strength to stand."

And he did go to bed, but only after writing to Marquis Simonetti about the martyrdom to which Judge Grassellini was subjecting a loyal and devoted servant of the Crown, to wit, His Excellency Giuseppe Vella, Abbot of San Pancrazio.

Chapter III

Toward vespers, a messenger from Monsignor Airoldi was dispatched to the house of Abbot Vella with a blanc-mange and sesame cookies, two delicacies that the Abbot doted on and that Monsignor often thoughtfully sent him; the man found two policemen stationed by the outer gate, both stiff with boredom.

"What's happening?" The messenger was alarmed.

"Nothing's happening. We're here to curry the cow," one of them answered; they were finding it a dull business to mind the stable from which the cattle already had been stolen.

"Where is the Abbot?"

"In bed, lucky man."

The outer door was open. The messenger went in, thinking he would leave the gifts in the antechamber if the Abbot really was in bed. All the doors were open, and from a room nearby he heard a hoarse rattle, a series of gasps, and broken speech. The man stood for a moment undecided, package in hand; he did not want to be indiscreet and enter the Abbot's bedroom, yet on the other hand those sounds struck him as coming not from a sleeping but from a dying man. Without putting his package down, he crossed the threshold into the bedroom. The Abbot lay in the half light of a deep alcove; his face looked like the face of a hanged man, the head thrown back against the pillows, the bulging eyes rolled upward until only the whites showed, the mouth sagging.

The messenger went over to the bed and called, "Abbot! Abbot Vella!," at which the rasping grew louder, the gasps more frequent. But the raving became more coherent; it had to do with the codices, the robbery, and certain people who wished him harm.

"Poor man, just see what a state they've brought him to," the messenger murmured. Then: "Abbot, I am here on behalf of His Excellency…Monsignor Airoldi, you remember Monsignor Airoldi?" as if he were speaking to a child. "He sent me with this blancmange and the sesame cookies you like…"

Irises flowered again in the white globes of the hanged man's eyes, which now rested briefly on the box that the messenger held out.

"Put it down here," the Abbot said, pointing to the night table by the bed. He fell to raving again.

And so, before nightfall, all Palermo knew that Abbot Vella stood at death's door. The news aroused conflicting reactions and opinions, interminable discussion, and even bets. Some said the illness, like the theft, was a fiction; some, on the other hand, believed it and were sympathetic; others attributed it to terror that the fraud, sooner or later, would be discovered, and still others to the unjust persecution he had suffered and to the robbery. That evening the police were obliged to rush to the Albergaria quarter, where a scuffle over Abbot Vella had broken out among the women, half of them taking his side and commiserating with him, the other half denouncing him; later they had to hurry over to the Kalsa, where some fishermen had taken to knives pro and con the authenticity of the *Council of Egypt.*

At the Conversation Club in the Cesarò Palace, opinions reflected more unanimous sentiments: at the moment these were indignation over Grassellini's tactics and suspicion of the Abbot. The suspicion was vague and hesitant, veiled by a respect that was paid ostensibly to the scholar, but in actuality to the even more formidable blackmailer who was securely ensconced still on the ramparts of the printed word and royal favor.

"The police, even the police are good for nothing," the Prince di Partanna was saying. "You report a theft and they come with a warrant to search your house! It's crazy!"

"He's a ruffian, pure and simple!" the Marquis di Geraci said.

"Yes, Grassellini's a ruffian by nature...He behaved the same way over the pettifogger, forcing through that farewell party for him! He tried the same tactics with the Prince di Caramanico, God rest his soul...A ruffian!...But what I wonder is, who called the tune this time?...Canon Gregorio? Impossible. The Marquis Simonetti? Unlikely. I don't think the Marquis has any interest in scuttling Vella, he's protected him too solidly. The Archbishop? The Archbishop doesn't care a hoot about this affair... Who, then?" Don Francesco Spuches's vacant glance traveled around the group.

"You, perhaps," said the Marquis di Villabianca.

"I?"

"I say you, meaning me, us, all of us – the nobility, in a word. Think for a moment what would happen if Grassellini were to produce proof, concrete proof, proof that would stand up in a court, of Canon Gregorio's suspicions and that Austrian's – what's the Austrian's name?"

"Hager."

"...Hager's suspicions that the *Council of Sicily* and the *Council of Egypt* are forgeries—"

"Impossible," Cesarò said.

"What do you know about it?"

"But men like Monsignor Airoldi, like the Prince di Torre-muzza – do you for a moment think that men like that have let themselves be taken in? And Tychsen, how do you account for Tychsen?"

"Let him account for himself... And as for Monsignor Airoldi and the Prince di Torremuzza, I take off my hat to their scholarship, but do you think Canon Gregorio and this Hager are any less learned? In any event, I am suggesting a simple hypothesis: the codices of Abbot Vella are forgeries... What happens if, on the one hand, Grassellini, and on the other, Hager, produce sure proof that the codices are false?"

"A cheap botch, that's what. People from here to the savages in the Americas will laugh themselves to death," Meli said.

"You only see the ludicrous aspect of my hypothesis, but

it is of a very definite, very practical interest for us. Suppose that Abbot Vella's codices are clearly proved to be forgeries. What would that mean for us?"

"Oh, I know, yes. The Royal Treasury would have to stop reclaiming all your lands for the Crown, as it has been doing on the strength of the *Council of Egypt*."

"That son of a— Excuse me, I mean to say that Abbot Vella has certainly aimed to ruin us," Spuches said in a sudden change of heart about the Abbot.

"What hasn't he handed over to the Crown through the *Council of Egypt*? Coastal holdings, farms, rivers, tuna concessions – things we've owned for centuries, things no king or viceroy has even challenged our right to," the Marquis di Geraci said.

"You see what a service Grassellini would be doing us?" the Marquis di Villabianca concluded.

"Who asked him to do anything?" the Prince di Partanna demanded; not even the rosy prospect that the codices might be proved false could dim his dislike for Grassellini. "Anyhow, you are only talking about a hypothesis. One thing is certain, however, and that is that Grassellini is committing an arrogant violation of a man's rights, and when I see a man's rights being violated, I see red."

"And the *Council of Egypt* does not violate people's rights, by any chance?" Ventimiglia asked.

"These are considerations to be put forward if and when the codices are proved false. But at the moment, what have we? A poor dying man," the Duke di Villafiorita said.

"A fine man," Ventimiglia said.

"A scholar," Spuches said.

A fresh wave of compassion for the Abbot surged up, and as if they were speaking of a man already dead, they launched into a melancholy recital of his many qualities. But a small crack had opened, and through it a different feeling was beginning to seep.

Chapter IV

After the strenuous night of the moving, Abbot Vella had made the monk swear on a scarred and battered crucifix that never would he breathe a word about it, and then he had given the man keys to a small country house he owned in Mezzomonreale: a most beautiful spot and a comfortable little house which very few, perhaps only the people who had sold it to him, knew to be the Abbot's property.

Had the Criminal Court dealt with the robbery case, it would have had great difficulty in laying hands on the monk; the informers of the Court of the Royal Patrimony, however, what with all the buying and selling, transferring and inheriting of properties that went on, had very sharp ears: one of them hinted to Grassellini that, who knows, the monk might be hiding out in the villa at Mezzomonreale that Abbot Vella had bought recently.

Grassellini dispatched every policeman he had available; it looked like a foray to capture one of the outlaw bands that roamed the area, which the police now and again undertook to track down entirely by way of gesture and without any success whatever. They surrounded the house and caught the monk – literally – on the wing: it was nighttime and he had thought he could escape by jumping out a low window.

Grassellini sent him in chains to the dungeon of the Vicaría. He had the man haled before him after two days of anguish and the vilest prison fare: by then the monk was ready to vomit all he knew of Vella's affairs except for what he had sworn on the crucifix to keep to himself; he truly feared that the very crucifix the Abbot had held before him would damn him in what, in holy terror, he called "the life everlasting."

The Judge grinned with baleful satisfaction to see the man standing before him wild-eyed and sprouting tufts of beard from his chin: the Vicaría had softened him up just enough. Grassellini attacked, using the information that the Abbot had astutely passed on about the monk's wantonness, but he spoke as if lechery were the only reason the monk now found himself afoul of the law.

"You had yourself a good time, eh?" Grassellini said; it was at once a question and a statement.

"Where? In the Vicaría?" The monk spoke in all innocence; he could not detect a shadow of a good time in his recent past, but Grassellini took it as insolent irony and turned red.

"Your good times at the Vicaría have not even begun!" he roared. "You'll see, you'll see!…I am asking you about the little games you played in the house of that saint who gave you hospitality, and who never even suspected! You playing the cock with women of ill repute while he was away from home, poor man, thinking all was well."

"Who told you?"

"Abbot Vella told me himself, and you know it's true. If you deny it, I'll fetch the woman you used to bring to the house and I will have her tell you to your face whether what the Abbot told me is true or not."

The monk had not expected any such black treachery from his patron, and he felt his whole world come tumbling down about his ears. "But that's an old story," he stammered.

"Old?" the Judge said more mildly.

"Two, maybe three years ago…"

"What happened, exactly, two or three years ago?"

"The Abbot came home when I wasn't expecting him, and he found me with Caterina, the girl from Ragusa…But I swear we were only talking—"

"Talking about what? Theology?"

"About things – oh, I don't remember now. But the Abbot, good Christian that he is, turned into the Devil himself—"

"Because he was not in the habit of indulging in that kind of conversation?"

"I can't say about that, in all conscience. Maybe, away from home…What do you expect? The flesh is weak."

"And then?"

"He was beside himself, he wanted to send me back to Malta…Then he thought twice: he said he would forgive me, but he made me swear that never again—"

"Why did he think twice?"

"He liked me, I believe."

"It certainly wasn't that he needed you. You were eating him out of house and home—"

"That's not so," the monk interrupted. "I worked like a dog."

"What kind of work were you doing?"

"The work there was to do."

"What work was there to do?"

"Copying...The copying had to be done right."

"Copying what?"

"Arab things."

"The codex – the *Council of Egypt* – did you write that?"

"I copied it. The Abbot used to give me a couple of pages a day and I would copy them...It took, I must tell you, all the skill, all the patience I had—"

"Those pages he used to give you, the Abbot wrote them, right?"

"I don't know."

"You are in a very unpleasant situation, you know. I am talking to you now like a brother: it will be much better for you if you tell me all you know without my having to ask."

"Maybe he did write them."

"Did he or did he not write them?"

"He wrote them."

"Good," the Judge said. "Good, good, good." He radiated satisfaction, he looked like quite another man. To the monk he said, in a most friendly way, "But you have produced a masterpiece, you know. The codex of the *Council of Egypt* is perfection, pure perfection."

"Well," the monk demurred, "some credit is due Don Gioacchino Giuffrida, too."

"And who is he?"

"The artist. The inscription on the first page, he did that."

"What inscription?"

"Where it says 'Gift of Mohammed ben-Osman' – But Your Excellency hasn't seen the codex?"

"Why no, my friend, no. I have been waiting for you, I have been waiting for you to tell me where I could find it, so I could have one little look, just one little look at it."

The monk was now thoroughly confused, but one shaft of light pierced his muddled brain and in it he saw the crucifix on which he had taken the oath writhing and bleeding.

"The Abbot keeps it at home," he said, "in a strongbox under his bed."

The tone of voice was so sincere that Grassellini believed him. Nevertheless, he kept on insisting, threatening. "It's not there any longer. The Abbot says maybe you stole it from him."

"Me? What do I want with the codex?"

"That's what the Abbot says…You have nothing to tell me about the disappearance of the codex? Mind you, the Vicaría—"

"The Vicaría is awful, but I cannot damn my soul for all eternity. Hell is worse than the Vicaría."

The Judge never knew that he made a serious mistake to interrupt the interrogation at this point: the monk was on the verge of telling him that he did not want to damn his soul – not, as Grassellini supposed, by telling a lie but by betraying an oath: and a short, a very short stay in the torture chamber might have persuaded him also to disclose the gist of his oath.

"You think so?" the Judge asked jokingly; he knew the Vicaría well, and he was more optimistic than the monk about the relative merits of Hell. He sat in thoughtful silence for a moment. "I know enough," he said to himself. "I've squeezed everything I can squeeze out of this fellow, but I still have not got hold of the corpus delicti, and that I must find."

"I want to say—" the monk began timidly.

"What?"

"About that woman...I want to say that I didn't do anything bad...We used to talk, we just talked. I—" and he burst into tears.

"Perhaps in your country you call what you used to do with Caterina from Ragusa talking. Do you know what it's called in my country? It's called—!" and he said it, crudely and with a laugh, whereupon the monk wept more copiously still. "But that is your affair. I'm a judge, not a father confessor."

Chapter V

With every passing day, the illness of Abbot Vella grew more serious. On the third day, he began to spit blood; on the eighth, he asked for the last rites, and all agreed that they should be administered to him. During the evenings, his bed was encircled by a crown of illustrious friends and fanatical admirers. During the day, his niece took care of him – in a manner of speaking, as the Abbot was up and about the house in a dressing gown, poised to slip into bed at the first alarm; never had he been more bursting with energy or more jovial, and he was, if anything, more gluttonous than usual. He had a few pangs of anxiety, of apprehension, true; but he had no doubt that the Marquis Simonetti would presently loose a thunderbolt on Grassellini's head. Assuredly the Crown could not afford the luxury of losing the *Council of Egypt*.

Monsignor Airoldi's concern for him had led to a visit from Meli, who was reputed to be a good doctor; Meli had listened to his chest, tapped him all over, and kneaded his belly, his back over the kidneys, and below his ribs – like iron, he reflected – until the Abbot had pretended to faint to make him stop.

While they were hurrying to revive him, Meli announced to those present that little or nothing could be done, Abbot Vella already belonged more to the world beyond than to this one; he was in greater need of God's mercy than of the services of a doctor.

"But what ails him?" Monsignor Airoldi had asked, for so far none of the doctors had been able to name the illness from which the Abbot was visibly suffering. "A stomach cancer, in my opinion...And the heart, too...Very weak...Can't hold out..."

You are a beast, a heartless beast, the Abbot was thinking, as with staring eyes he asked, "What's wrong? What's wrong?," exactly like someone who is regaining his senses and does not realize what is going on. You are a beast. Or you're doing this on purpose because you've caught on and want to turn my game against me – which was not impossible, given Meli's fondness for practical jokes and the bitterness he had shown toward Vella more than once for having managed to snatch the rich abbacy of San Pancrazio from under his nose. Then a doubt wormed its way into the Abbot's mind: he really might have a cancer somewhere inside him without realizing it, everyone knows how those things go, and a doctor is a doctor, after all. A shadow, a mere shadow of apprehension that served rather than marred his purpose of the moment.

The viaticum was brought to him with great solemnity. The priest who heard his confession and gave him extreme unction told Monsignor Airoldi, "We are witnessing the death of a saint," and said as much to others, with the result that Canon Gregorio and his partisans found their shoulders pinned to the wall: how fight a dying man; what's more, a dying saint? One syllable of doubt about the illness or, even worse, about the saintliness, and most people would have branded them as beasts, the most repulsive kind of wild beasts – jackals and hyenas.

The situation was of the Abbot's own choosing, but there was one drawback about being moribund: he did not know what Grassellini was up to or what point his investigations had reached. Monsignor Airoldi and his other friends carefully avoided the subject: How can one speak of unpleasant things to a man who is bound to life by a mere shining thread of consciousness? At times, the Abbot essayed a "Have they found the *Council of Egypt* yet?" or "The Lord has seen fit to nail me to this bed; otherwise, by this time I would have given Hager all the satisfaction he wants…Modesty apart, I would have made him eat his words." Whereupon everyone hastened to tell him that he must not trouble about such things, he must think only about recovering his health.

He was given a nasty turn by Baron Fisichella in this connection. One day when he asked, "Have they found the *Council of Egypt* yet?" the Baron, to comfort him, said yes they had found it. Cretin. The Abbot nearly choked, and the Baron got a fearful dressing down from Monsignor. "Don't you see that this poor man is dying from grief at having lost the codex?… One should use some forethought, some care in giving him such news, even if it were true. And you rush in like a clumsy—"

"But the news I gave him was good news," the Baron said, in self-defense.

"Even good news can kill a man who is lying between life and death."

Anything but good news, the Abbot was thinking, and he began to breathe freely again. Worse news than that I hope I never hear...But they won't find it, as God lives they won't find it. Grassellini can turn himself inside out looking for it, and Gregorio and that Austrian with his fresh sausage of a face can turn themselves inside out too...All of them, inside out...In the meantime, Marquis Simonetti...

Marquis Simonetti had done what he had to do: he had sent a dispatch in which he instructed the Criminal Court to take the investigation of the theft under its jurisdiction and ordered Grassellini to relax his efforts; he had sent a letter to the Abbot in which, to extricate him from the machinations and persecutions of the barons, he invited him to Naples. But letter and dispatch arrived in early February, by which time the Abbot had wearied of playing the dying man; news of Grassellini's disgrace spread throughout Palermo together with word of Vella's sudden recovery, which the Abbot attributed to a nocturnal sweat that cleared away all feverish humors – a sweat so unexpected and abundant, so prodigious, that he could not but render thanks to St. John the Hospitaler, whose devotee he was and who had undoubtedly intervened to save him.

Two days later, the Abbot ventured out of the house. He had himself driven in a carriage through the city. It was one of those iridescent Palermo mornings, the clouds a shelving deep blue and russet. He rejoiced in the sun, the air, the warm Norman stone, the red Arabic cupolas, the aroma of seaweed and lemon in the market; he felt restored to life, as if he really had triumphed in a strenuous struggle with death; his senses were sharper, freer, more subtle; the world was more delicate, all matter more pure.

The goal of his long, meandering drive was the Royal Palace, where Monsignor Airoldi had arranged a meeting with the Lord President of the Kingdom, functioning for the moment as Viceroy, Monsignor López y Royo.

The Viceroy received him cordially and spoke affably with him. He was not a man to be disturbed by the suspicion, which flourished even in Palermo, that the Abbot was a forger; on the contrary, the suspicion inclined him to be sympathetic. He was a man of sordid avarice and obscene vices, sinister and soiled even in things that at that time were readily overlooked, and particularly in what the Marquis di Villabianca termed "venereal peccancies." Whether the Arabic codices were faked or authentic he considered no affair of his: let the nobles and Simonetti, Monsignor Airoldi and Canon Gregorio, dispose of that question; his concerns of the moment were the interdependent ones of keeping an eye on the Jacobins and holding out to become viceroy in fact.

Conversation touched on the Abbot's illness and his miraculous cure, and then turned to those very Jacobins.

"The Prince di Caramanico, estimable man, let them multiply like rabbits so that now I have quickly to man the ramparts. I must be constantly on guard, ferret out danger wherever it raises its head...A task that leaves little time for sleep, I assure you...He loved the French" – this was said with the same horror that other people injected into the charge that he, Monsignor López, was stealing from the construction funds for the Duomo – "and let's not even speak of Caracciolo, who positively adored them. Mine has been a heavy inheritance, a sorry, a most sorry inheritance...The Kingdom is thick with Jacobin weeds, and it's fallen to me to uproot them." He held out his hand and clenched his fist, as if he were pulling a nettle up by the roots.

The Abbot was startled: in less than a month, the situation had begun to reverse itself; he could not imagine what reason, what developments could have placed such a brutal, contemptible man in a post that he had seen occupied for more than ten years by intelligent, free-spirited, subtle, and tolerant men.

"And the books, the books are like weeds too," Monsignor López continued. "You have no idea how many there are here already, and how many keep arriving – by the crate, by the cartful! But however many come, that is how many are burned by the executioner." He was flushed with satisfaction, as if the reflection of the flames played over his face and glittered in his eyes.

"Good books are few, very few, these days," Monsignor Airoldi sighed.

"Few? There are positively none...All rubbish that aims to turn the world upside down, to corrupt all morality. There's not a scribbler alive today who doesn't want to have his say about the organization of the state, the administration of justice, the rights of the King, and the rights of the people... That's why I admire men like you. You spend your time looking for things in the past and get along in blessed peace with the present. You aren't itching to turn the world upside down. I admire you, I truly do admire you for it."

Chapter VI

Grassellini had no sooner tapered off his investigation than a dispatch arrived from Acton countermanding the dispatch of Simonetti. The government in Naples must have been in a turmoil, as bad as any butcher shop, den of thieves, whorehouse. The Abbot suffered a slight relapse, for the dispatch labeled his alleged theft a lie and strongly hinted to Monsignor Airoldi that he, as conscience and judge for the monarchy, should be watching, investigating, and unmasking Vella. This was as much as to tell poor Monsignor Airoldi to prepare the rope by which he himself would be hung – hung by a base trick, derision, and disgrace.

Two days later, a third dispatch, this one from the Office of the Secretary of Justice and Clemency, restored things as Simonetti had first arranged them. The Abbot's condition took a sharp turn for the better, so much so that he decided to confront Hager at a meeting to debate publicly the question of the authenticity of the codices. Hager had already studied the Codex of San Martino – that is, the *Council of Sicily* – and he was just about to send off his verdict in black and white to Naples; it was a judgment to raise the hair on one's head.

But he felt obliged to accept the Abbot's challenge, thus, he thought, seizing the lesser evil. Not to accept would hand Vella the victory that by accepting he might be able instead to snatch from him, even if the meeting would offer a margin of advantage to the Abbot, who would surely be as adroit in discussing the codex as he had been in forging it.

Named to preside over the debate were Monsignor Granata, Bishop of Lipari; Canons De Cosmi and Fleres: a priest by the name of Lipari; and Cavaliere Speciale; all five as innocent as lambs in the matter of Arabic.

Hager opened the discussion, saying that he had examined the Codex of San Martino from the first to last page, and with a clear conscience could state that it had been entirely – and recently – mutilated and corrupted. Nonetheless, he could state under oath that he had managed to decipher these words, "The man sent by God and whom God favored"; he had identified names of Mohammed's family scattered pretty much everywhere, and found references to places and things that unquestionably belonged to the history and legend of Mohammed, from which he had justifiably deduced that the codex was a biography of Mohammed and had nothing whatever to do with Sicilian history.

The Abbot was watching him with icy disdain, and when Hager stopped speaking, he grimaced in disgust.

"Signor Hager is an educated man, he comes from a nation of educated men. I," he closed his eyes in humility and resignation, "I am only a poor translator, quite unenlightened in matters of culture. From childhood, I have been drawn to the Arabic language. I spoke it and studied it in Malta; I can say that I know it better than I know our vulgar tongue. That is all…But I wish to ask Signor Hager," and he raised his voice for effect, "what opinion he holds of Professor Olaf Gerhardt Tychsen: whether he considers him an impostor, an impostor like myself" – he looked about him, smiling with melancholy scorn – "or rather a man who possesses a full and absolute knowledge of the Arabic language and of Arabic history."

"Professor Tychsen is a great Orientalist, but—"

"He is not an impostor?"

"He is not an impostor, but—"

"Do you mean to say, then, that you know more than he?"

"Not that at all, but—"

"Do you mean that he has been deceived by me?"

"Yes, that's it."

"So that I, then, know more than he?"

"No."

"He more than I?"

"Yes, but—"

"He knows more than I, yet I have been able to deceive him…Does this seem to you possible?"

It did not seem possible. The five judges – one could read it in their faces – did not believe it. And from the public in the rear of the hall came a burst of applause.

"Let us leave Professor Tychsen alone," Hager said. "Particularly since he will, I am sure, have occasion to revise his opinion."

"You believe that his opinion will then coincide with yours?"

"Yes."

"So that you, in effect, know more than he does!"

"Put it as you like…Meanwhile, here we have the Codex of San Martino; we can discuss it concretely."

"Let us discuss it," the Abbot said.

The Codex lay on the table, and Hager opened it. "I would ask Abbot Vella," he said, turning to Monsignor Granata, "to point out to me the name Ibrahim ben-Aglab, which he has translated a hundred times."

Monsignor Granata turned the Codex toward the Abbot.

Vella turned two or three pages and laid his finger on one spot. "Here."

Hager leaned down, then straightened up, red with anger. "But here I read Uqba ibn Abi Muait!"

"And who says you should not?" the Abbot asked with an icy smile.

"Then find me another place where the same name appears!" the Austrian exploded.

The Abbot turned a few more pages, and pointed.

"An Nadr ibn al Harit," the other man read, and shouted, "But, my God, this is too much! Compare them! Compare them! Ibrahim ben-Aglab is written one way in one place and another way in another place! Compare them!"

The five judges bent over the Codex; the letters were, in fact, different. They turned perplexed faces to the Abbot.

"Signor Hager," Vella said ironically, "has a truly admirable enthusiasm for things Arabic, but they call for much study, much patience…His youth alone tells us how far he still is from his goal…I envy him his youth, I do not envy him his knowledge. However, I do not doubt that with time he will be able to attain to the erudition in which for the moment he is almost entirely deficient…You see, gentlemen, this Codex is written in Siculi-Arabic."

"I've never even heard of Siculi-Arabic – except from you, of course."

"You see? You have never even heard of it. And I dare say that you have never heard of the many, the countless forms of Kufic characters—"

"I have heard of them. I know them."

"Then why are you so astounded that the name Ibrahim ben-Aglab should appear written once in one way and again in another?" The tone was that of a grieving parent.

"Let us proceed to the test of approximation," Monsignor Granata said, opening the translation of the Codex of San Martino that lay before him. Turning to the Abbot, he said, "If you please, open the Arabic text to page twenty-four… There, translate that."

The Abbot translated with remarkable assurance: every word he pronounced corresponded exactly to the version that Monsignor Granata had before him.

"That will do," Monsignor said, after a while, and to Hager, "It matches, word for word."

Hager snickered.

"You translate it," Vella invited him.

"Just like that, on the spur of the moment?"

"I do understand," the Abbot said, "how this or any other

moment might not be convenient," and while the hall rocked with laughter, he was tempted to make a grand gesture: to recite to all those stupid oxen, friends and foes alike, the true translation of page twenty-four: "Abd al Muttalib called him Mohammed after a vision he had. He believed that in a dream he had seen a chain of silver, which…"

Chapter VII

"I have a notion that that Hager is right," Di Blasi said suddenly, interrupting his two Benedictine uncles, who were happily recapitulating the events of the evening's confrontation. He was accompanying them back to San Martino, for it was quite late; the closest friends of the Abbot and Monsignor Airoldi had stayed on after the conference for supper at the latter's house; and what with excellent food and fine old wines, they had doubly savoured the evening's triumph. Because the Abbot's victory was their victory: it was a victory for Monsignor Airoldi, who had invested his name and money in the venture: a victory for Giovanni Evangelista Di Blasi, who, on his own, had published a tract against Gregorio and in defense of Vella; and a victory for Francesco Paolo himself, who in the preface to *Pragmaticae sanctiones regni Siciliae* had quoted the Codex of San Martino as a source of legal precedent.

During the evening, the two Benedictines had noticed that their nephew was silent and rather abstracted: but they knew that ever since the death of his wife, after less than two years of marriage, and now from worry over his mother's health, he often lapsed into short spells of despondency, when he became touchy and even irascible. They were not prepared for his concocting any such wild suspicion as this. They were scandalized.

"How can you think such a thing? After such complete, such brilliant proof?" Father Salvatore said.

"My experience as a lawyer," Francesco Paolo said. "I have seen truth twisted, I've seen a lie take on the semblance of truth…When I heard Hager say that he could not improvise a translation of the Codex, suddenly I understood which side the truth lay on…And then I remembered something, a tiny thing of no importance whatever, from about ten years ago – I mean that at the time it seemed unimportant, but now I see it in context."

"What are you talking about?" Father Giovanni demanded.

"How is your mother?" Father Salvatore asked; he ascribed his nephew's recollections and suspicions to some family worry.

"As usual. She's sick, but she won't rest, she goes on taking care of me, the house, all our business affairs—"

"A determined woman, your mother," Father Salvatore said.

"A determined woman, yes…But I would like to understand this: How can such a black suspicion about that poor Abbot Vella even occur to you, to you of all people? You have been friends for ten years and more, solid warm friends…And now, of all times, when you should be beside yourself with joy . . . Did you see Gregorio, the state he was in? He looked like a codfish three days out of water…At a moment like this, when we should be putting up a statue to Abbot Vella, you begin to suspect him!" Because he had risked defending Vella and hated Gregorio, Father Giovanni felt personally wounded and betrayed by his nephew's suspicions.

"It's just an impression. I could be wrong," Francesco Paolo said soothingly; he already regretted having started the discussion.

"That I can believe. It's your work, it makes you blind. You lawyers are so used to switching truth and falsehood, to clothing one as the other, that at a certain point you can't distinguish between them… Like Serpotta, who dressed whores in expensive clothes and used them as models for his statues of Virtue."

"And splendid statues they are," Francesco Paolo said to divert his uncle to a fresh subject.

"Once the breath of God cleansed them," Father Giovanni said.

If God doesn't soon blow a breath of air on Abbot Vella's codices, the lawyer thought, I'm afraid they'll come to a bad end. Not to purify them, as Uncle means about Serpotta's work. In that sense, in the sense of art, as a work of art, an invention, a creation, quite possibly they are already pure. If the Abbot really did make them up out of nothing, then he has created one of the great works of imagination of the century. But if they're to be accepted as authentic, he does need this breath, he needs the miracle of the water being turned to wine. Di Blasi was smiling over such ideas, and smiling a bit at himself, too. He had fallen for the Abbot's game, had he not? But he was not making a tragedy out of it. In a text that competent authorities had declared authentic, he had found certain points of civil law and, as a student of law, he had made a passing reference to them. That was all. But Professor Tychsen, what a blow it would be for him! And for poor Monsignor Airoldi. And for his uncles. But especially for Tychsen; he, the great Orientalist, who had in effect helped the Abbot put his scheme over. The whole thing seemed incredible, really, and yet there was no mistaking it; in Hager he had heard the unequivocal accent of passion, of truth; the agonized impotence and repugnance of the honest man confronted by the overbearing lie; he had watched Hager retreat in what had seemed confused guilt, but had actually been despairing innocence. The lie is stronger than the truth, he thought. Stronger than life, even. It is found at the very root of beginning life, and it is still sprouting forth leaves in the afterlife. The dark tossing of the trees along the San Martino road was grafted onto the more obscure leafy crests of falsehood. Roots, leaves! He was often irritated to find himself thinking in metaphors. The little child lies as naturally as he breathes, and we believe him. On the say-so of some Jesuit priests, we believe that man is a moral savage. And we believe that truth came before history, and that history is a lie. Instead, it is history that redeems men from falsehood and error and brings them to the truth, individuals and nations both...And to himself, in ironic self-congratulation: Since you have believed in Rousseau, it is only right that you should find your requital in Abbot Vella. Yet the young lawyer felt bewildered, as if some sudden obstacle, some unforeseen collision, had exploded into a curse. The fact is, Voltaire is more useful to you today...Perhaps Voltaire is *always* more useful...But even so not as useful as you would like. You would like their ideas – Voltaire's, Diderot's, Rousseau's too – to be *in* the revolution, to be a part of it, instead of stopping short at the threshold.

"Here we are, San Martino," said Father Salvatore.

Di Blasi stepped down from the carriage also. He kissed his uncles' hands and wished them good night.

"Don't let your ideas get too wild," Father Giovanni urged him: he was alluding to Abbot Vella.

The young man stood for a moment looking out over the mysterious, formless countryside; in the flickering light cast by the torch the groom was holding high beside him, it looked more formless and mysterious still.

He climbed back into the carriage, and all the way to Palermo and through the night into dawn, his thoughts were wilder by far than any Father Giovanni feared he might have. But they were not exactly concerned with Abbot Vella and his Arabic codices.

Chapter VIII

The report from the commission that had presided over the test, including a meticulous transcript of the evening's proceedings and a statement of the judges' conclusions, which overflowed with enthusiasm for the ability and probity of Abbot Vella, had been sent off to Naples at about the same time as Hager's critique, to contradict, to annihilate the latter. Yet the Abbot felt weary and depleted; he was the actor who has played the leading role throughout the long run of a successful comedy, the same character, the same mask, evening after evening. It was not that he was confused or hallucinated or awash in a double identity, because such a state of mind had not yet been invented; even had it been fashionable, the Abbot would have thought the *paradoxe sur le comédien* more appropriate to his personality and situation, but then that, too, was unknown at the time.

Furthermore, it would be a gross error to attribute his weariness to any stirring of conscience or remorse. On this score, the Abbot was as cold and immaculate as a snow field on the Madonie Mountains. Those ten fat tomes of fraudulencies sat as lightly and joyously on his conscience as

indulged his contempt for others

a bright, fluttering feather; in a word, he felt spotless. But if he was to savor his euphoria to the full, he needed something; he needed a chorus of his victims, so to speak. He had so indulged his contempt for others that had he not acted as he was now about to do, there would have been nothing left for him but to despise himself as well; his reasons for so doing were far removed from eternal verities or the then absolute moral certainties. But better not complicate matters: let us simply say that Abbot Vella was sick to death of everything.

And so, come the *aequinoctium vernum* of 1795, as the astronomer Piazzi turned away from his telescope in the observatory of the Royal Palace, with the rivers of stars that had poured into his eyes now flowing into the sea of sleep, Abbot Vella was throwing his windows open to the mild morning air. He felt rested, serene, redeemed. He was forty-four years old; he had an iron constitution, a quick mind; and just as the spring was now returning in glory, he felt that he too had come to a freer season in life and to fresh vigor.

He decided to take a bath, a phenomenon no less rare than those Piazzi spied on in the equinoctial heavens. He heated water in great copper pots and poured it into a small gray marble tub; he undressed and immersed himself, bent over in three, like one of those American mummies that a Jesuit priest in Malta had once shown him. A bath was death in miniature: his body melted, his whole being dissolved into suds of sensation. He was deliciously aware that he was committing a sin. On such occasions, he always remembered the warning of an early Church Father: with his amazing memory, it was as if he had the printed page before him; he repeated the words now, translating them from the stern Latin in which they had been written: "If you cannot indeed avoid immersing yourselves naked in water," the Church Father had said, "do not touch your body while you are wet." The Abbot was mindful of the prohibition, and his hands dangled over the edge of the tub like broad Indian-fig paddles. But a bath was a delight, nonetheless. As the Arabs very well knew, he reflected. For a moment, a woman's glance flashed from behind the dry and thorny bramble bush of the Latin, languidly curious about his naked body. The Abbot closed his eyes. He drifted into a light sleep. And her hands, or someone's hands, stirred the water that embraced his body. How lucky that the Church Father had foreseen no such thing as this.

When he emerged from his bath, he felt the need of coffee, a drink rarely taken and always prepared and savored with gusto. He was leisurely about dressing and setting to rights all the confusion occasioned by the unusual event of a bath, and then he went out. He stopped by his niece's house and collected the *Council of Egypt* from the top floor, where it had been hidden, together with other papers. He called a sedan chair to take him to the home of Monsignor Airoldi.

Monsignor was still abed. Half asleep as he was, he recognized the codex. "Don't tell me a thing," he said. "First let's have coffee, and then you tell me the story, blow by blow… I'd given up all hope. This is a miracle."

The Abbot drank his second coffee of the day.

"Now tell me," Monsignor said, settling back against the pillows the servant had arranged behind his back.

The Abbot laid the *Council of Egypt* on the bed. Eagerly Monsignor drew it up on his knees and opened it.

"I should like Your Excellency to examine it closely," the Abbot said.

"What's happened?" Monsignor was alarmed. "Have they damaged it?," and he began to leaf feverishly through the codex.

"Not at all."

"What then?"

"Your Excellency must be good enough to examine it closely … With the kind of attention, I mean, that Your Excellency has so far not deigned to give it."

"But …" Monsignor looked up at him, uncomprehending, waiting for an explanation.

"It will be enough if Your Excellency will hold any page – here, this one – up against the light … The weave of the paper … The watermark, that is …"

Monsignor did so: and since his eyesight was weak and, at the moment, rather blurred, he read, "a-o-n-e-g."

"Your Excellency," the Abbot said quietly, indulgently even, "Your Excellency has read it backward. The watermark reads 'g-e-n-o-a.'"

The Bishop's jaw dropped; like a dying man, he exhaled a whispered "Genoa."

"This paper," the Abbot said, "was made in Genoa, I assume about 1780. I bought it here in Palermo a few years later."

"Lord Jesus," the Bishop said: he fell back on his pillows, wild-eyed and open-mouthed.

Abbot Vella stood looking at him impassively, a cold smile on his lips.

"You have ruined me," Monsignor said finally. "I should have you arrested."

"I am at Your Excellency's disposition."

"At my disposition?" Monsignor's expression was that of a nursing infant who has had the bile of a hedgehog forced down its throat: every line in his face was contracted around that one center of bitterness, which was his mouth and the words it uttered: "You have murdered and buried me, you have carved my epitaph of shame on stone... At my disposition!"

"Your Excellency's indignation is sacred for me, and I am ready—"

"This is a comfort, a comfort indeed," Monsignor said ironically, and at last he exploded: "Get out! Get out before I have you whipped out like a dog!"

imposture, fraud

Chapter IX

"It's true," Di Blasi said, "every society produces the particular kind of imposture that suits it best, so to speak. Our society is a fraud, a judicial, literary, human fraud – yes, I would say human too, for it is fraudulent in its very essence. So our society has produced, quite simply and naturally, a reverse fraud—"

"You are squeezing philosophy out of a common crime," Don Saverio Zarbo said.

"Oh no, this is no common crime. This is one of those facts which help define a society, a historical moment. If culture in Sicily were not, more or less consciously, a fraud, if it were not a tool in the hands of the barons, and therefore an imposture, an endless imposture and falsification of reality – well, I tell you this, Abbot Vella's adventure would have been impossible. I'll say more: Abbot Vella has not committed a crime; reversing the terms, he has produced a parody of a crime, of the crime that we in Sicily have been committing for centuries."

"I don't understand you."

"I'll try to make myself clear – and be clearer in my own

thoughts, too. You remember the Prince di Trabia's speech on the agricultural crisis? The crisis, the Prince said, is caused by the peasants' ignorance—"

"Not only by the peasants' ignorance, as I remember."

"Right. He pointed to other causes, but the principal one, according to him, is the ignorance of the peasants. Therefore, he says, let us educate the peasants. Now I ask you: Where do we begin?"

"On the land, of course. Teach the peasant how it must be worked, what are the best methods, the best tools, which crops are best suited to a particular soil and terrain, how one lays out an irrigation ditch—"

"And his rights?"

"What rights? Whose?"

"The peasant's right to be a man, for one… How can you possibly expect a peasant to do an intelligent man's job without at the same time giving him the right to be a man? A well-cultivated countryside is the image of applied reason: it presupposes that the person who tends that land is effectively sharing in universal enlightenment and universal rights… Now, do you believe that a peasant on one of your estates really shares in any universal rights when a letter from you to the overseer is enough to have him thrown into jail? Just two words: 'So-and-so is to be jailed for good and sufficient reasons of my own.' And that man will stay in jail so long as it suits your convenience… These things still happen, the law of '84 notwithstanding."

"What you are saying is very important," said Don Saverio,

nuisance

"and interesting too, very interesting. But I can't help always seeing the reverse of the coin, the amusing side. You make me think of the Baroness di Zaffú. She was only fifteen when she happened to notice that a peasant is a man, and she never changed her mind about that even when she was an old lady."

"According to Montaigne, if I'm not mistaken, the discovery that a peasant is a man was made by the nuns in some convent or other hundreds of years before the Baroness di Zaffú."

"Amazing. Montaigne, eh? One of those Frenchmen of yours, I suppose…I say, things are going rather badly for those people up there in France, don't you think?"

"Not for Montaigne, in any event," Abbot Carí said with an ironic cackle, "not for Montaigne."

"I've never had the pleasure of reading him," Don Saverio said. "But Montaigne aside, those Frenchmen are beginning to muck— Excuse me, to be a nuisance, in a word."

They were beginning to be a nuisance, a bit more of a nuisance than Don Saverio and the Sicilian nobility were inclined to put up with, and a little less of a nuisance than Monsignor López y Royo, to consolidate his position as future viceroy, would have liked.

In the Di Blasi home, at the periodic meetings of the Sicilian Academy of Rhetoric, arguments over the French were becoming more heated than the discussion of Sicilian poetry, to which the Academy was dedicated. In fact, the idea of reviving the Academy had occurred to Di Blasi, whose father had at one time supported it, while he was casting about for some instrument to advance the political aims he was secretly

envision a Sicilian republic
Crush the old order by force
revolution!

pursuing: that is, through dialect poetry and research to create a more unified dialectology, to give concrete and democratic meaning to Sicilianism, to Sicilian nationalism, which most people cherished only in the abstract; and, at the same time, to develop cautiously a program for propagandizing such ideas and winning converts. Years of uneasy concern for his country had finally brought Di Blasi to envision a Sicilian republic: the death of Caramanico, with the subsequent elevation of López, was now pushing him into action. There was no hope of returning to the spirited days of Caracciolo, no hope, even, that the mild era of Caramanico would continue: within a month, within a year, Monsignor López would have become a kind of Spanish viceroy; with him in office, the barons would revert to their old arrogant ways and recapture the privileges that Caracciolo had unraveled and nibbled at.

There was no more opportune moment to attempt to crush the old order by force: a viceroy whom the nobles despised and whom the people hated, who was a sharp man in disreputable dealings but absolutely lacking in the intelligence and courage needed to face a critical situation; discontent among the urban workers and the peasants; troops stationed in Palermo and throughout the island, few in number and of by no means certain loyalty; and the French, who were shifting their armies and fleet so that no one could tell where they would strike when, thus keeping the Naples government in a state of severe anxiety. On the other hand, there was France. To Di Blasi and to those few friends who had joined with him in the conspiracy, France was both idea and passion; the French Revolution, the French Republic, and the armies of Revolutionary France spelled the hope of prompt and fraternal aid to the future Sicilian republic. Yet that same France posed the threat of failure. The name France alone awakened echoes of hunger and suffering among the people; memories of their long-ago Angevin rulers and the bloody massacre known to history as the infamous Sicilian Vespers had been quickened in recent times by the Duc de Vivonne, Marshal of His Most Christian Majesty Louis XIV. The people constantly harped on their hatred of the French and the Jacobins. Every misfortune was attributed to the French and their local friends: the war and the revolution that they were bringing, or threatening to bring, to Sicily; the anger of God that they had provoked; black blight among the corn; phylloxera in the vineyards; overabundant rainfall; drought.

Pastoral letters in which the Jacobins were called horrible wild beasts, bloodthirsting and voracious – panthers, wolves, bears, sly and malevolent foxes – thundered in the churches of the Kingdom; the people prayed to the Madonna and to the Saints to keep the French far from their shores, as once they had prayed to fend off the Turks, and to wipe out and send to the Devil, for suitable torture, those fellow countrymen who secretly belonged to the infamous Jacobin sect. Yet Francesco Paolo Di Blasi was attempting to organize a Jacobin revolt.

He was encouraged by the faraway examples of Squarcia-lupo and D'Alesi, who had been successful at least at the outset, and by the recent revolt against Viceroy Fogliani – by all the popular uprisings, that is, which in the more or less remote past a handful of men had been able to spark in Palermo. He believed that the very elements that those movements had carried within them as the germs of failure, or that had made them easy to suppress, destined for success the movement that he captained. It would not be a riot that would break out on April 5, but a revolution fired by a great idea, and it would not be limited to the city of Palermo, but would spread throughout the island. The participation of the peasants was a primary, an essential, condition for the success of the revolution: the conspirators gave more time and energy to agitating out in the country, arousing the peasants in the name of the hunger and oppression they suffered, than to stirring up the servile, treacherous city.

But while men talked in Di Blasi's house of the French and the spurious Arabic codices, and while Abbot Meli was reciting an anti-Vella poem to just a small circle of friends, so as not to hurt the feelings of his host and his host's uncles, who had been supporters of Vella, in the Church of San Giacomo alla Marina, the eighty-year-old priest Pizzi, palpitating with joy and horror, was listening in his confessional to a revelation of the conspiracy.

Chapter X

When young Giuseppe Teriaca came out of the silver-smith's shop where he worked, the time being almost two o'clock in the morning, he found the Church of San Giacomo still open; he walked over wearily to undo the knot he had felt tightening inside him for several days. Also, it was near Easter and, as the Church asked, at least at Easter a man should confess and take Communion; all the more so if he felt trapped in a plot in which he could not tell good from bad. At almost the same moment, Corporal Karl Schelhamer of the Foreign Regiment began to feel about the army of which he was part very much as Teriaca was feeling about the Church.

The result was that Brigadier General Jauch and Father Pizzi appeared simultaneously at the Royal Palace with, respectively, the corporal and the silversmith in tow.

Had the watching eye of the world and his own age allowed, Monsignor López would have scampered up the curtains, the draperies, and onto the chandeliers, such was his joy to hear their revelations. The group was in the salon that, taking its name from the still recent frescoes by Giuseppe Velasquez, was beginning to be called the Salon of Hercules; Monsignor

had transferred himself and his surprise guests to this room
from the little study where he had first received them, judging
the salon more likely in size and acoustics to shield such a
fearsome and secret business from the trained ears of the
servants, by whom he was hated and whom he hated in return.

The silversmith and the corporal had had from Monsignor
the formal promise of immunity that Father Pizzi and
Brigadier Jauch each had dangled before their eyes; now they
were talking, and it was a pleasure for Monsignor to listen.
Also listening were the Royal Procurator, Damiani; the
Prefect, the Prince del Cassaro; and the Captain General of
Justice, the Duke di Caccamo. If Damiani's joy equaled Monsignor's, that was justified by his occupation; the other two
were listening with mingled disgust and dismay, particularly
the Duke di Caccamo. Indeed, when Monsignor López turned
and ordered him to proceed to arrest all those whom the
spies' evidence had implicated in the conspiracy or merely
cast suspicion on – with special attention and care to be taken
with Di Blasi – the Duke, his face drawn but his voice quietly
decided, said that he really did not feel he could arrest Di Blasi.

Monsignor bridled. "Why not?"

"Because he is my friend," the Duke replied.

"Ah, he's your friend! The King, God keep him, will be
happy to hear that he is your friend," Monsignor said with a
ferocious sneer.

"I can do nothing about that," the Duke said. "I have never
approved of his ideas, and I believe that there can be no
doubt about his guilt, precisely because I know his ideas and

his character... I will say more: I detest his crime. But he is a friend."

"And in what is he your friend? Do you go to women together?" Women were forever brushing their way through Monsignor's thoughts. "Play primero? Go on picnics?"

"And study Latin, study Aristotle," the Duke said; the edge of his scorn for Monsignor was flawed by the emotion these memories aroused.

"Foolishness, rubbish," Monsignor said, and then in a persuasive, paternal voice, "You are the Captain General of Justice. Your duty, my dear Duke, is very clear; you cannot do less. Suppose that the Procurator and the Prefect and everyone else invested with authority were to entertain the same feelings for Di Blasi as you. What would happen? The enemies of God and Crown here in Palermo could make merry when and as they liked, and the King, God keep him, would be in a fine quandary for having put his trust in you and in your loyalty... At any moment, the end of the world will be upon us, the wrath of God will be breaking over us, and here you sit quietly and..." His voice rose and cracked in anger. "And the King, God help him, what is he to you? Something to be kicked around?"

"Your Excellency can order me in His Majesty's name to do anything else, to put a bullet through my head even, and I will do it – here, in front of Your Excellency."

"I cannot order you to do any such thing, but I leave it to you to weigh some other opportunity for just that. What I can order you to do is perform your duty and make the arrests.

We will see later what they think about all this in Naples. Meanwhile, arrest Di Blasi—"

"I will go," Damiani said.

"If you happen not to be a friend of his, if you will deign to," Monsignor said scathingly. The Duke of Caccamo had blasted his euphoria. Why should a man deny himself the pleasure of annihilating another man, if his mind were not tainted by the same filth, his heart corrupted by the same guilt? Might this mass arrest bring out something about the Duke di Caccamo?... What a joke that would be. But the Duke truly did detest the Jacobins, almost as much as Monsignor López y Royo detested them; only, unlike Monsignor, he had friends. As he rode home in his carriage, he was moved by the image of himself behaving as a loyal friend, until Monsignor López's threats began to make that image twitch with apprehension and fear, even as the Duke contemplated it.

Meanwhile, Damiani was putting the entire police force of Palermo on an emergency basis; some were unleashed to descend on the silversmith's quarter to capture the four companions whom Teriaca had informed on; others went to the barracks of the Calabrian Regiment to arrest Corporals Palumbo and Carollo, denounced by Schelhamer; still others hurried to arrest Master Builder Patricola, whose name had come up in the vague testimony of the two informers; this was the Patricola who in the eyes of his contemporaries enjoyed the merit of having raised the cupola above the Norman Cathedral which today makes us regret their not having arrested him earlier and for less idealistic crimes.

The cream of the police force Damiani reserved to follow him on the more arduous maneuver against Di Blasi. For with Di Blasi one had to move carefully on account of his rank and his reputation, but especially so as not to allow him time to destroy documents that, as a top figure, if not actually the leader of the plot, he in all probability had somewhere in his possession.

Di Blasi was not at home. After the meeting of the Rhetoricians, he had gone in the company of Baron Porcari and Don Gaetano Jannello, who were part of the conspiracy, for a stroll along the Marina, for the night was very mild and people were resuming, as they did every spring, the habit of an evening promenade by the sea. Damiani was glad of it; he posted his men around the house, and himself hid in the doorway of the house opposite, ordering the night watchman to leave him a candle and betake himself to bed. Everything was much easier this way. And indeed, after perhaps an hour, as the servant who walked a few steps ahead of Di Blasi, carrying a torch, was about to open the door, the lawyer found Damiani by his side and the police surrounding him; he had a moment, barely a moment, of confusion, like an attack of vertigo. But swiftly, lucidly, he saw that the game was lost and his own life finished, his destiny fulfilled.

"If, in the circumstances, my word were worth anything, I would assure you that you will not find any papers in my house worthy, so to speak, of your attention." The light of the torch flickered over the deepened pallor of his face, but he was calm, and he spoke in the low, distinct voice that Damiani had always admired in him during trials and in conversation, and with that vein of irony which people who keep watch over their feelings inject into everything they say. "I should like not to disturb my mother at this hour and in the company of these gentlemen." He gestured toward the police.

"I am sorry," Damiani said, and he was truly sorry, for in the land of Sicily, a mamma establishes communion even between State offenders and Royal prosecutors.

"Come," Di Blasi said, moving up the stairs, preceded by the servant who was lighting the lamps, and followed by Damiani and the police. He walked into his study. There stood his mother, motionless in the middle of the room, her hand to her heart, a waxen statue in which the one sign of life was the feverish anxiety of the eyes. The smell of burned paper filled the room. When Damiani had come looking for her son and not found him, she had sensed unerringly why they were searching for him and had gone down to his study to burn the papers she believed might compromise him. But compromise him in what connection? She knew nothing about the conspiracy; nor was there in the study a single piece of paper that had to do with the conspiracy. Who knows what she's burned, the young man thought, and now this fellow is growing suspicious. Damiani was sniffing the air like a hound dog.

Di Blasi was exasperated. These mothers of ours! They foresee everything, know everything, and only complicate everything! His annoyance enabled him to assume a stiffness, an appearance of coolness, that he needed at that unnerving moment.

"These gentlemen must waste some of their time looking about here. It's their duty... An official search, in a word."

Donna Emmanuela nodded; she was looking into her son's eyes and shaking her gray head to say yes, she understood, she had always understood. Destiny, the son was thinking, yes, that she has understood. Her own destiny... How to accept sorrow and death, to which her life has always been bound. But Donna Emmanuela understood also that at this moment her son wanted to send her away: a man has the right to be alone when he faces his own fate, when he must confront betrayal, police, death. She said, "I'm going to the next room. Send for me if you need me."

She turned to leave. "Thank you," her son said. During the years that remained to her, these were the words that would blossom in her heart, in a long, an endless, mad colloquy. She paused by the door for a moment. Don't turn, don't turn around, her son prayed silently. His heart was thudding the way it sometimes did in dreams, when he would cling to a slender branch or thicket above an abyss. He closed his eyes; when he opened them again, she was forever no longer there.

Damiani had rushed to the drawers of the desk. Not that he was convinced he could find anything, but duty is duty. He looked through the letters, one by one; he scanned them as if reciting Ave Marias, but he was disappointed in their contents. The police were wheeling around him like a merry-go-round, not knowing quite where to lay their hands. Finally, the Procurator barked, "The books! Clear the shelves. Do you expect me to wait here all night!"

Di Blasi was sitting almost in the middle of the room, facing the dark walnut shelves from which the police now began to pull books by the armful. They piled them on the floor, near him.

"Books, these are your books," Di Blasi said to himself; he had to mock, to wound himself. "Old paper, old parchment. Books were your passion, your mania. But these people care less about books than mice do; at least, mice eat them. But what about you, now? What value can books have for you any longer? Were they ever of use to you, except perhaps to bring you to where you are now? You would have had to leave them behind sometime in any case; now or in twenty years, leave them to some relative or friend or servant... Yes, you could have left them to young Ortolani, perhaps; he loves them as much, maybe more than you do...No, not more than you do. He loves them differently, as a scholar. No danger of his ending his life as you are about to end yours... But you cannot give them to him now; they belong to the King you have plotted against, which is to say, they belong to the police. Look at them carefully – it's for the last time...Here are the pamphlets in which you wrote about how all men are equal...De Solis, who made you dream of America...and the Encyclopedia, Volume One, Volume Two, Three..." He counted them, volume by volume, as the police stacked them on the floor beside him. "And Ariosto—'O great conflict in the youthful heart,/ The thirst for fame and thrust toward love contending!'...Not those lines, not those lines now!...And Diderot, five volumes, London, 1773." He stretched out his foot toward the nearest pile, to kick it over. Damiani, who never let him out of his sight even as he read the letters he kept pulling from the desk drawers, jumped to his feet in alarm, and ordered the police to leaf page by page through the books that Di Blasi had knocked down.

Imbecile, Di Blasi thought, don't you understand I am beginning to die?

Chapter XI

"The matter is not at all clear. Abbot Vella came to my house and told me a story that is neither fish nor fowl. I do believe all this furor of suspicion and attacks and tests has clouded his mind, poor man." Monsignor Airoldi looked like a man risen from the dead; in his own fashion, he was relating to anyone who might be curious – and numerous people were most curious – what had happened between him and Abbot Vella. It is well known that walls have ears, and all Palermo was already agog over the face-to-face exchange they had had in the privacy of the Bishop's bedroom. Monsignor had avoided leaving the house for several days; now, what with the discovery of the Di Blasi conspiracy, he hoped that people would have forgotten the story of the falsified codices and the Abbot's confession, and so had ventured to go out; after meeting only three or four people, he was convinced that he had made a mistake; people were all absorbed, yes, by that tremendous plot but, like Phaedrus' dog, they were prepared to drop that bone in order to sink their teeth into Monsignor's spindly calves.

"Yes, he confessed that he falsified something," Monsignor

admitted, "but I couldn't gather exactly what ... Perhaps the *Council of Egypt* ... In any event, you can be sure that the *Council of Sicily* is authentic. You had proof of that, after all."

He was negotiating with the Abbot to insure that he would not confess to having corrupted the Codex of San Martino, because the title page of the Codex of San Martino bore the legend: "*Codex diplomaticus Siciliae sub saracenorum imperio ab 827 anno ad 1072, nunc primum depromptus cura et studio Airoldi Alphonsi archiepiscopi Heracleensis*." He should own only, if at all, to the falseness of the other, in which the Archbishop of Heraclea's scholarly care was not officially involved. In exchange, the Abbot could count on Monsignor's indulgence. But the Abbot was saying neither yes nor no to this; he kept to his house, and when Monsignor's emissary would go to see him, he would change the subject or, smiling fixedly, would sit listening in silence. From what had happened that other morning and what his emissary reported back to him, Monsignor was indeed inclined to believe the Abbot truly mad.

"In a word, I know less than you," Monsignor said, "and then, what with all that's going on ..."

As punctual as swallows, the ladies and gentlemen of Palermitan high society returned every year to the Conversation Club in the Piazza Marina: the same names, the same faces; the same threadbare comedy of gallantry and gossip was now, however, complicated by recent events. We might better say enriched: most persons relished both developments, for an indolent society delights in terrible or shameful events, especially if the protagonists belong to that same society and rank. However, this year the advent of spring coincided with Holy Week, so that the band was absent from its platform, the ladies were dressed in somber colors, notably purple, and the amiable reunion of these fine folk was slightly subdued by a note of official mourning.

"It's not worth discussing," Monsignor Airoldi said, "especially since I myself have not managed so far to get a clear idea of what happened. In my opinion, his illness dealt that blessed Abbot such a blow that he's become a bit odd...But we have more serious things, much more urgent troubles..."

"Santa Rosalia has protected us," the Princess di Trabia said.

"Just think, today is the day the uprising would have broken out," the Princess del Cassaro said; as wife of the Prefect, she was the best informed among the ladies.

"I should say that Jesus Christ has protected us," the Marquis di Villabianca said, "since this is the week of His Passion...I should say that the inspiration to confess came to that young silversmith, that young Teriaca, directly from Jesus Christ...Oh, the Lord has been most merciful toward us; if we stop to consider our sins, our vanities—"

"Oh yes, most merciful," Monsignor Airoldi said.

"The Lord," Don Saverio Zarbo interrupted, "had what you might call a direct interest in the plot. You know that their criminal plan of action marked the churches to be sacked first."

"They thought it out very clearly," the Prefect's wife said, "very shrewdly, because all the churches set out their most precious treasures on Holy Thursday."

This was a propaganda finesse of Monsignor López; he was terribly afraid that the populace might rise up, and he had invented this detail to appeal to popular sentiment.

"The fact is," the Prince di Trabia said, "that we have been nourishing serpents in our bosoms. But I can say this with a clear conscience: I never did like that Di Blasi."

"That's true. Your Excellency was never on intimate terms with him," Meli said.

The Prince did not appreciate this testimonial overmuch, and he turned a face of chill reproof on Meli. "You, however, liked him very much."

Meli excused himself. "Our only connection was that we shared a love of poetry."

"And you believe that he loved poetry? Where in a heart as black as his could there be room for a love of poetry?"

"He did love it," Abbot Carí said, as if to himself; he shook his head, his thoughts far away. "He did love it."

"Senile old man," the Prince murmured.

And Meli said, "Oh no, my dear Abbot, as the Prince so rightly observed, we can now say definitely that he did not love poetry, he could not love it. That was all so much dust in people's eyes, in the eyes of gullible people like me."

"You are the one who does not love poetry," Abbot Carí said, looking at Meli with dim eyes. He got painfully to his feet and, leaning on his cane, walked uncertainly away.

"I? I don't love poetry! Did you hear him, the poor old fool?" He glanced around in outward amusement but with, deep inside, a flicker of terror. "I write poetry, and people will be talking about my poetry when there'll be no trace of your name—" he was shouting after Carí, who was already some distance away – "no trace, not even on the marble they'll plant over you when you're dead."

"Don't quarrel with him – his head doesn't work very well any more," the Prefect's wife said comfortingly.

"But there's one thing I can't understand. You," Prince di Trabia said to Meli, "used to visit him, you were very close… Because you both loved poetry, of course… And Your Excellency also," to Monsignor Airoldi, "had frequent contact with him—"

"On questions of scholarship, only on questions of scholarship…"

"Questions of scholarship, naturally… But," the Prince continued, "there must have come some moment when, to eyes as versed in human nature as yours, Di Blasi must somehow have revealed his true nature—"

"Never," Meli said.

"Never," Monsignor said. "He had his own ideas, of course, but that they would ever lead him even to conceive of such infamy—"

"Ideas, you say?" the Marquis di Geraci burst out. "From now on, if you think you see anyone having ideas, run him through with your sword! We have escaped by a hair, do you know that? If Providence had not intervened, they'd be playing *bocce* with our heads this minute."

"Oh, Heaven!" The ladies shuddered.

"Ideas! You're so right. But" – the Prince di Trabia assumed the expression of a man about to reveal a daring proposition – "I have worked out what you might call an idea about ideas. And it is this: ideas come in the door when money leaves."

This met with general approval.

"And all things considered," the Prince continued, "the ideas over which so much ink is spilled are not so different from the ideas of a common thief. Only, the common thief has no idea that he has ideas" – he was pleasantly surprised by his own word-play and wanted to enjoy it to the full – "and if he had any idea that the deeds he commits sprang *from* an idea, and that that idea is defended in books, and that a whole nation, a great nation like France, has begun to put that idea into practice ... Well, what difference would there be between the bandit Testalonga and Lawyer Di Blasi?"

"None. Each one of them was after what belongs to me," the Marquis di Geraci said.

"What belongs to us," the Prince corrected. "But Testalonga, poor fellow, acted with more discretion, I would say – precisely because he had no idea that he had ideas."

"Yes, yes, yes," the Marquis said; his attention was beginning to wander from the effort of following the Prince in forming an idea about ideas. "But the important thing is, we have brought all these people to a halt. And this would be a good opportunity to clean out the whole stable, Abbot Vella included."

"That is quite another matter," Monsignor Airoldi said timidly.

Chapter XII

"You've written how torture is contrary to law, contrary to reason, contrary to man's nature, but a shadow of shame will hover over what you have written if you yourself do not resist it now... *Quid est quaestio?* That is the point at issue here. You've already answered what it means to put a man to the question – how bland, how legally correct it sounds! – to torture him, but you've answered in the name of reason, of human dignity; now you must answer with your body, suffer in your flesh and bones and nerves, and still not speak... 'Put the slaves to the question!' *Servos in quaestionem dare, ferre – ah, judges and their Latin!*" The heads of his judges floated before him in the fog of his own pain. "*Quaestio!*" Pain was seeping into his brain like ink, blinding him. His body was a twisted, tangled vine of pain: incommensurable, heavy with gobbets of blood. Gobbets of blood, the dark blood of man. "Put a man to the question, torture him, and he loses all sense of his own body. You... you would not recognize your own body now in the engravings of Vesalius or in Ingrassia's iatrology, and even less in the Creation of Adam, in Monreale. Your body has nothing human about it any longer; it is a tree of blood ... The theologians should have to undergo this: they would finally understand that torture is against God, that it destroys the image of God in man ..."

Suddenly he sank into a sea of darkness, his heart fluttering like a broken wing. When he could see once more, he was again before the judges' table; he felt the ground beneath his feet; a wave of pain, hot and urgent, beat only against his wrists. "You've had the first strappado; there will be more. What were you thinking before they let you drop?" He raised his eyes to measure the distance he had fallen – two ells, perhaps less.

"Well?" Judge Artale said.

"Nothing," Di Blasi said. "I've nothing to add to what I've already stated. It is my fault that the people whom you have arrested were involved in a conspiracy without even knowing its real aims. There were no others ... I realize that it was madness, I am profoundly sorry that others must suffer on my account ... I took advantage of their trust in me, and of their ignorance—"

"I agree as to the madness," the Judge said, "but not too fast. I cannot believe that your hope of success was based on a dozen or so people: there must be others you do not want to name, perhaps people who were active in the plot and who were over you ... And what about the French? There must have been some promise on the part of the French government, some guarantee—"

"I have never had any connection, not even a vague connection, with French agents ... I was the head of the conspiracy, I managed to mislead only the few people you have captured. I am sorry you do not believe this; it will be a waste of time."

"I am sorry, too," the Judge said.

Once more the pulleys screeched, and his body, dark and amorphic, burgeoned with agony. "Don't make me black out!" he prayed; he was praying to the dark nature of the blood, of the tree, of stone; to the dark God. "Judges who believe in the *question* also believe that witcheries exist that help one resist it: *multi reperentur qui habent aliquas incantationes ut multos habui in fortiis in diversis locis et officiis.* What they don't know is that the sorcery is simply thought: in essence, the magic is only thought." He looked down at the judges' heads below his feet, and at their table and their papers. "You must keep thinking; if you want to hold out, you've got to keep thinking…Two hundred years ago or more, they gave the strappado to Antonio Veneziano: 'Seven strappados he was given, and he withstood them.' You must withstand, too. He was a poet, a man of more delicate constitution than you, more susceptible, and yet he withstood… for a pasquinade against the Viceroy, and you, instead, for a crime against the Crown…Remember one of Veneziano's poems, any one… Say it out loud, say it!…I can't, oh, I can't." A spasm of pain shattered the detachment he had been able to sustain by talking to himself as if to a second person: the executioner had jerked on the rope. "Now they're going to let you drop," he told himself. "Keep hold of yourself, keep—" But he plummeted down with a groan.

The Judge got up from the table. He walked around and stood in front of the prostrate body: he was considered a good man, a humane judge; the fact that someone should stand up under torture he held to be an offense to his own sensibilities, a rebuff of the mercy he was accustomed to extend even to criminals. So his next question was angry: "You had been informed of Colonel Ranza's arrival?"

"Colonel Ranza. Who is he?"

"You know perfectly well who he is, and we know too, fortunately."

"I've never heard the name…According to you, who should have informed me of his arrival?"

"Your friends on the Committee of Public Safety. Colonel Ranza is their agent; and we know that he has been sent to Sicily to reach an agreement with you."

"You know more about it than I."

The Judge returned to his chair. He sighed. "We have other means," he said. "Don't force me to have recourse to them…Don't force me."

"I know. Night after night with no sleep allowed, torture by fire…I know. Human stupidity has proved extraordinarily inventive in devising torture. I know. And I don't expect to be spared any of them. It may be that you will succeed, that you'll make me admit I was waiting for this Colonel Ranza with open arms. I hope not, but considering the torture you promise, I cannot exclude it. But at this moment, during this short relief, I want to tell that I have never even heard the name of any Colonel Ranza. I give you my word, man to man."

"Man to man!" The Judge's voice was menacing now. His hand shook with anger as he reversed the small hourglass he kept on the table; to the executioner, it was the signal for the third strappado.

Chapter XIII

Word of Di Blasi's arrest reached Abbot Vella via his niece. While she was washing pots in the kitchen or arranging what few things needed to be put in order, she would give him a report on what was going on in the city: usually the Abbot was lost in other thoughts and did not hear her; only now and then he caught a name, a phrase in the endless monologue, and if it aroused his curiosity he would question her. And so it was that day.

"...and the leader of the band was a lawyer, Don Francesco Paolo Di Blasi."

The Abbot caught the name as someone walking along a dusty street turns up a shining coin or fragment of glass with his toe. "What band? And what has Di Blasi to do with it?"

"He headed a gang that believed neither in God nor in the Saints. They were planning to rob the churches of every last treasure, and to do it today, Holy Thursday...But they arrested them."

"Di Blasi? It can't be. Who told you this foolishness?"

"All Palermo is talking about it, and it's true as Gospel. And Nino, who could put out a newspaper with all he knows about what's going on, this Your Worship knows, Nino told me that the lawyer has been locked up in Castellammare and has had the strappado already." Nino was her husband; as the Abbot supported his family, he gave himself exclusively to skimming news among the coachmen, watchmen, and sacristans, and to frequenting houses of prostitution and taverns.

"It can't be, it can't be!... You know Nino better than I. He's likely to mistake a lantern for a wineskin, especially if he's drunk his quota for the day."

"But everybody is saying it."

"Tell me again everything you've heard, step by step."

The niece repeated her version of events, and her version was the version of Monsignor López. The Abbot was not convinced, but he admitted there must be some truth in it.

Later in the day he got a more formally coherent account from Monsignor Airoldi's messenger, but the conclusions seemed no less inadmissible. One thing was certain, however; Di Blasi had been arrested; the Abbot felt that he should express his dismay by some token of solidarity and friendship. For the first time in his life he perceived, he shared, the agony of another. A weakness, a surrender, but in this particular case he did not regret it, even as he admonished himself to keep his distance in the future from connections that might involve similar feelings. "But there is no danger of that," he told himself. "From now on, you will be as lonely as a leper." It was said without drama, rather with pride, as he surveyed the landscape of his own solitude.

He hired a carriage and had himself driven up to the

Monastery of San Martino. The evening light shifted as purple-black clouds were cleft at intervals by the blood-red setting sun. The trees shuddered, and so did the Abbot, murmuring superstitiously, "Holy Week weather," for he was thinking how such weather always accompanies direful deeds and tragedies.

When he asked at the porter's lodge for the Di Blasi brothers, Father Giovanni and Father Salvatore, the men who were gathered around talking glanced at each other and whispered among themselves; after many if's and maybe's, one of them brought himself to go up to see if… He came back presently to tell the Abbot that Father Salvatore, Father Salvatore only, was awaiting him in the library; Father Giovanni, poor man, simply did not feel it in him to see the Abbot. Ah, ah, ah, the Abbot thought. The library! Once more he saw the scene where his plan had first taken shape: the Ambassador from Morocco leaning over the codex, Monsignor Airoldi eagerly waiting for his comments. Who knows, if Father Salvatore is receiving me in the library, at the scene of the crime, he may be doing it on purpose?… But no, he must have many other things on his mind.

Father Salvatore was working. He rose and came to meet his caller. They shook hands without speaking. Then the monk motioned the Abbot to sit down, and he also sat down.

"Perhaps I am disturbing you," the Abbot said, "but I could not help coming to see you the moment I heard the news, because for your nephew I have—"

"I know, I know," Father Salvatore said, and the Abbot thought that he detected a tremor of impatience.

"A man of intelligence and feeling, of whom there are few. And I absolutely do not believe what they are trumpeting all over the city – that he planned to sack churches, steal holy vessels…All malicious slander, circulated by people who did not know your nephew or who have some interest in spreading such rumors."

"You're right. I don't believe he would ever have stooped so low, although, you understand, there could be people in the group who thought differently. But he, no, I don't believe it…The fact is, however, that he had an even worse plan; he wanted to subvert public order and proclaim a republic… A republic, dear Jesus, a republic!"

"But—"

"That does horrify you, doesn't it? You would never have believed he was capable of conceiving of such a monstrous plan…I understand you; I would applaud your feelings, if only the tie of blood that binds me to him, and the memory of my poor brother—" He pulled out a handkerchief and mopped his eyes – "Ah yes, you too have the right to be horrified, *even you*."

That's the first slap, the Abbot thought. "Not at all. I do not feel I have any right to judge him, much less to be horrified. On the contrary, I must tell you that a little while ago I was amazed and incredulous, but now I see it clearly: I did not believe your nephew was capable of plotting to pillage churches, but if you tell me he was preparing a revolution—"

"That doesn't surprise you?"

"No."

"I see ... Actually, that is the way it is: the people closest to a man are the last to recognize that he is mad, especially if the madness grows slowly – the way, living together all the time, one doesn't notice age creeping over the faces of others ... He seemed to me to be a man of sound sense, and yet he was mad, mad ..."

"You have misunderstood me. I mean that for him the republic was an ideal, and so I am not surprised that he would try to make it a reality."

"Ah." The monk's eyes narrowed as he scrutinized the Abbot's impassive face. There was a long silence.

"If," the Abbot resumed, "if it is possible, given the way things have gone, to discuss it at all, one could ask whether the moment was right, whether his resources were adequate and his judgment balanced – whether, in sum, given the time and the circumstances, it was not madness, in the usual meaning of the word. Folly. But that is very far from saying that your nephew is mad."

"Ah ... Would you, by any chance, hold the same ideas? About a revolution, a republic?"

"For me, republic and monarchy are the same brew, the same swindle. Whether there be kings, consuls, dictators, or whatever the devil they may be called, matters less to me than the course of the stars. Perhaps less ... But revolution? I confess I feel differently about revolution. That out-with-you-and-in-with-me ... what shall I say? I like it. The powerful are unseated and the poor rise in triumph—"

"And heads fall," the Benedictine added ironically.

"Well, yes, a few," the Abbot said composedly. Suddenly he felt like a boy egged on to defiance. "A few. After all, what is an unthinking head worth?"

"So it isn't true, you aren't totally indifferent to the form of the State, or to the methods and the men of government. If you make a distinction – a distinction, I might say, as thin as the edge of the guillotine's blade – between heads that reason and heads that do not reason, it is clear that you would prefer to be governed by heads that do reason; that is, by heads that *in your opinion* reason. I imagine it is a foregone conclusion that the others would fall." Father Salvatore's voice faltered with indignation.

"Yes," the Abbot said, "perhaps you're right… Actually, I have never given any thought to these things… Eh, yes, you are quite right."

A thought crossed the Benedictine's mind that, for the form it took, would require him that evening expressly to ask God's forgiveness: This man is trying to squeeze my balls… But he was mistaken; the Abbot was genuinely astounded to discover that he cared about things he had always supposed remote, things even positively repugnant to him. Indeed, he had had occasion more than once in recent weeks to be astounded by his response to the conversation of others or to thoughts that germinated in his own fertile solitude. A memory from childhood had come back to him as a parable to express what was happening to him: it was from the days when he was a little boy, and he had begun to attend catechism class; other small boys filled the oratory benches, thick as swallows.

After a week, his mother took a fine comb to his head, for red marks had begun to glow all over his scalp, and she discovered lice. Her horror at verifying this – his mother was a woman whom poverty did not prevent from worshipping cleanliness even to excess (the Abbot did not resemble his mother overmuch) – still echoed in his ears and conscience: "They've got you crawling with lice!" It was a warning and an accusation. The lice of faith. Now the lice of the mind. Quickly, as always, he drove the image, the memory, the parable, away; he had come now to the sin against friendship.

The Abbot had been lost in thought. He collected himself to find the Benedictine's unfriendly, inquisitorial eye upon him. He felt intimidated, confused. "That's the way it is," he said. "A person never thinks about some things until suddenly there they are, staring him in the face."

"Your hands were full of very different things," Father Salvatore said sourly.

Again the childish impulse of defiance welled up: "Yes, all that blessed work of falsifying the codices—"

"You speak about it like that? To me?"

"How do you want me to speak about it to you? It's the truth."

"But do you know something? Crazy as my nephew is, he was the first person to suspect your swindle."

"Really? When?"

"The evening you massacred Hager, that very evening."

"I am so pleased," the Abbot said. "I am truly pleased."

Chapter XIV

"When peasants mention feet, they use the expression 'speaking with respect.' Now you can do the same; you have cause." Stretched out on a cot, he squinted down at his feet, which were hanging over the end of the cot, not because it was short, but so that they would not have to touch it: they were shapeless feet, like the lumps of earth that cling to uprooted bushes; bloodied, encrusted lumps of meat. They stank of scorched fat, of rotting flesh.

As he lay looking down, the distance between eye and foot seemed unreal, and his pain was also remote. He thought how worms live buried in moist earth: cut them in two, and both ends continue to live; he felt like that, one part of his body living only by pain, the other by his brain. Only man is not a worm; feet belong to the mind, too: when the judges called him again, he would have to reconquer the part of his body that now seemed so far away, cut off almost; he would have to order his feet to set themselves down on the ground and to move. Before the judges, it would be up to his feet to express his serenity and strength of mind – feet that already seven times had endured torture. That nineteenth verse of the

Inferno had helped him to withstand it – *Allor fu la paura un poco queta/ che nel lago del cor m'era durata* – and other poetry of Dante, Ariosto, Metastasio: all of them forms of that sorcery the judges so rightly believed in. The jurists Farinaccio and Marsili, who had written on torture, had helped him too; racking his memory for their definitions and their stupid commentaries had helped. For, after enduring the strappado five times, and sleeplessness for forty-eight hours, and having his feet burned seven times, he could now affirm with greater awareness that those who had conceived torture and those who upheld it were senseless men: they were men who conceived of man and of their own humanity as the wild hare or the rabbit might. Pursued by man, by their own humanity, they found their senseless revenge in the eternal *question* – jurist, judge, executioner alike. "Perhaps not the executioner. Perhaps the executioner, who is considered a vile thing because he must perform acts of cruelty, may at least derive some humanity from them, since they must make him realize how vile he is."

He was feverish. And he was desperately thirsty. Now and then he glanced at the jug of water, but he did not move. He would not move until the judges called him again. The agony of standing on his feet would be more dreadful than his thirst; because the others were not there, he spared himself. The others. The police, the judges, the executioner. But now his mother also belonged to the world of the others, "the world where people walk, where feet tread the earth without pain." Torture had given absolute definition to his solitude: "others" were henceforth different from him even in this: they were able to walk. Even his mother, torn by grief for him as she was, had at least this ability in common with torturers: she could move from bed to chair, from one room to another. And that was how he saw her, wandering through the dark, silent house, a figure of *soledad*, "like the Madonna in the Spanish church. We call her the Grieving Madonna, but Spaniards speak of *soledad*; for them, sorrow and mourning mean solitude…But my mother's solitude is not mine: physical pain, the mutilation or diminution of the body gives solitude an absolute quality; it severs the slender bonds that even in the soul's deepest despair we are able to maintain between ourselves and others…You said soul…Can you really still think about the soul's reality when torture has shown you that your body is everything? Your body has resisted, not your soul; and your mind, which is body, has resisted. And very soon, body and mind… '*Mas tú y ello juntamente en tierra en humo en polvo en sombra en nada…*' Another poet, but one you never loved very much. Now you love them all; you are like a drunkard who can't tell one wine from another. The fact is, you now love life as you never loved it, never knew how to love it. Now you know what water is, and snow, and a lemon – every fruit, every leaf you know now, as if you were inside them, as if you were their essence." These were the images of his desire, of his fever: the cherries that were now beginning to redden among the deep green of the leaves; the oranges that were becoming scarcer now, yet had a sweeter, stronger taste, like late grapes; and lemons, lemons and snow, glasses

heaped with powdered ice, and the sharp scent of fruit...
He saw the Cloister of San Giovanni degli Eremiti, the citrons
so thick and heavy that they were caught up in small nets
to prevent their falling from the tree. The Cloister of San
Giovanni, the church, the red cupola, the dense trees with
their fragrant burden. "You will never see them again." The
red cupolas. The Arabs. Abbot Vella. "He spelled out the fraud
of life, after his own fashion... With zest... Not the fraud of
life, the fraud that is in life... Not in life... Yes, yes, *in* life..."
His thoughts swirled away on a wave of fever. "Yours was a
fraud too, a tragic fraud." No matter how far he wandered,
he always returned to the men whom he had dragged into
the conspiracy and, with compassion and remorse, to those
who had accused him before the judges. Those who had
withstood, like him, shared human dignity: Giulio Tinaglia,
Benedetto La Villa, Bernardo Palumbo: he could not, it would
not be just, to pity them, to feel remorse for their fate. That
Corporal Palumbo: his steadiness, his silence, his scorn for
the judges; who knew where... what experience, those things
had come from? He regretted now that he had not known the
man better, had known nothing of his life, did not remember
who had brought him into the conspiracy, did not even
remember his voice: a dark, taciturn man. "Sometimes you
were suspicious of him because he was so closed and because
he was a corporal, which you thought something lower than
a simple soldier. And instead..."

But it was the others, the others, the others who tormented
him: the ones who had been afraid, who had trembled and

implored and denounced. "No use your trying to hide behind your solitude: it isn't real, you aren't alone. You're with them – their cowardice keeps you company. Because if they are cowards it is on account of you, and the day will come when they will realize this and will despise themselves…But now you can do nothing more for them than you've already done during the hearings. There's nothing left for you to do for them except to hope that their sentences are light, or that they are released even…And why should they not be released?" He began lucidly to elaborate a defense until an aching, congealing sleep flowed over him, but in his sleep he continued to grasp at the echoes and fragments of that defense.

Chapter XV

Baron Fisichella, who shuttled between Monsignor Airoldi and Abbot Vella, arrived at the Abbot's house early in the morning, surprisingly, for usually he appeared in the afternoon; he was out of breath, perspiring, and upset. He said straight off that he had bad news, but he took some time to come out with it bluntly. "They're going to arrest you. They're going to arrest you before evening."

The Abbot was unmoved.

"Monsignor is sorry, he's very bitter…He really did not expect this."

"I expected it," the Abbot said.

"But, heavens above, couldn't you disappear, hide out somewhere?"

"I have no wish to move, I am tired… And then, call me crazy if you will, I also want to see how it's all going to end."

"Well, I can tell you that, and I'm just an onlooker. People are saying, 'Let's see how this imbroglio is going to end, let's see how Abbot Vella will wriggle out of it' – but you're in it up to here!" He raised his hand to the level of his mouth to indicate the depth of the water in which the Abbot was about to drown.

The Abbot shrugged indifferently.

"I don't understand you," the Baron said. "By my word of honor, I don't understand you."

"Nor do I," said the Abbot.

"But look – prison!…Doesn't that make any impression on you, doesn't it frighten you?"

"I have never tried it."

"And I've never tried— Excuse me, that would be too unseemly…I've never tried…You understand me…Eh, do I make myself clear?"

"What you have never tried has nothing to do with man – because I do understand what you mean…But prison, yes, prison does have to do with man, indeed I would say that prison is in man, in his nature."

"Yes, yes, yes," the Baron said on an ascending scale, but meanwhile he was thinking to himself, Let's let him have it, then. This fellow is stark, raving mad. He got up.

"Do I seem mad to you?" the Abbot asked.

"Not at all, not in my wildest dreams…But listen to me. What I am about to say to you now is the last warning Monsignor Airoldi will send you: stand firm on the Codex of San Martino. You did not corrupt that text, you translated it word for word. Do as you like about the *Council of Egypt* – say that it's false or not, as you please…Even if you confess that it is false, you will still have ways of justifying what you did, of attenuating your guilt. Because, in effect, the *Council of Egypt* was born from seeds in a wind that favored the things Caracciolo and Simonetti were trying to accomplish here; you might say that it was born at their suggestion, veiled or open, as you prefer. Hold to these positions, in a word, and Monsignor Airoldi will not fail you."

"We shall see," the Abbot said.

"You know the saying, 'God helps those who help themselves'? In this case, if you help yourself, you will be putting Monsignor in a position to help you."

"We shall see," the Abbot said again.

They bade each other good-bye. The Abbot stood at the top of the stairs as the Baron went down. Before he reached the door, he turned around for a final farewell.

"Excuse me," the Abbot said. "I forgot to ask you about Lawyer Di Blasi. Is there any news?"

"No news. Just that he's cooked."

"Cooked?"

"He wouldn't talk. They did use fire, you understand…"

"And then did he talk?"

"No. But by now they have all the information they need, they're ready to go after him tooth and nail. His sentence will be something to remember." Clutching his throat, he mimicked what – the gallows.

"Is all this already known for a fact?"

"Of course," the Baron said. He waved and went off.

The Abbot returned to his chair by the window. He sat there for hours, hours on end, like a paralytic.

The cruelty of the law, the practice of torture, and the

atrocious executions, several of which he had witnessed in the past, had never disturbed him: he had assigned such things to the category of natural phenomena or, to be more precise, had thought of them as natural corrective measures, not unlike pruning vines or trees, and just as necessary. He knew that there was a book by someone called Beccaria that opposed torture and the death penalty: he knew of it because Monsignor López had only recently ordered any copies of it to be sequestered. Also, he was familiar with Di Blasi's ideas on the subject. But so many fine ideas are abroad in the world; the only trouble is that they have a double aspect, the other being desperate and violent. Now, however, he had to envisage a person whom he knew, a man whom he esteemed and loved, wracked by torture and condemned to the gallows; suddenly he felt how infamous it was to live in a world where torture and gallows were a part of the law, of justice; his revulsion was physical, he felt as if he were about to vomit. "I'd like to read Beccaria's book. Monsignor Airoldi is sure to have it…But they're going to arrest me. Perhaps I won't be allowed to read books at all, much less if they're proscribed…Who knows? – Will they take me to the Vicaría or to Castellammare? I forgot to ask the Baron. Castellammare, perhaps; Monsignor Airoldi will have put in a good word." Prison truly did not intimidate him; he had lapsed into a state of total indifference toward comfort and the pleasures of life; he had a far stronger appetite for showing the world what luminous proof of imagination and ingenuity he had given in the *Council of Sicily* and the *Council of Egypt*.

In a word, the writer in him had shaken off the hand of the impostor and broken free; like one of those shining, black, mettlesome Maltese horses, the writer was off at a gallop, dragging the impostor behind in the dust, his foot caught in the stirrup. Also, he was accustomed to live in the company of his own thoughts. He followed public events, past and present, in order to deduce their meaning and portent just as once he had derived lotto numbers from people's dreams. "Life really is a dream. Men want to be aware, to understand, and they do nothing but invent cabalas. Every age has its own cabala, every man has his own. And out of the dream that life is we form constellations of numbers to play on the wheel of God or the wheel of Reason. All in all, we are more likely to end up with winning numbers on Reason's wheel than on God's: we play out the dream of winning within the dream of life." His old occupation as numerist supplied him with the words to express, at least approximately, his own cabala, a faint, wavering, fugitive cabala that flickered out in superstition.

And there were memories. Within the dream of the present, he now also dreamed the past. He saw Malta on the rim of sea and sky, in a golden haze of memory. Suddenly, it leaped into his eye as into the lens of a telescope, and into his heart: he saw the tapering campaniles, slender as minarets; the low white houses, the belvederes; from the bastions of the old city, he saw the sweep of fields between Siggeui and Zebbug, with their yellowing harvests of Majorcan wheat and the intense green of the sulla and the joyous purple-pink of its blossoms, the whole veined by low white walls. "*Issa yíbda l-gisemín*." The jasmine was coming into bloom, and poured its perfume over terrace and street. Old men savored it as they sat on soft rush *suffahs* smoking their eternal pipes; the women worked at their little looms, weaving lengths of light cotton; indolent young men plucked fitfully on their guitars, the suspended chords spinning a melody through the languid air. At evening, the guitars struck up like crickets, and up from the port floated the songs of the sailors – Sicilian, Greek, Catalan, Genoese – eloquent of far places and homesickness. As the boy listened to the drunken tales of the sailors, the world unfolded before him like a fan: he discovered the vast and varied adventures that new places offer to even the poorest man, and he saw that the only possibility for the poor man to pluck the pleasures of life lay in changing scenes. And it happened that sometimes he would surprise the sailors in secret places along the shore, locked in dark embraces with the Veneres of the waterfront, heavy women, misshapen like their prehistoric forebears from whom Malta was said to have taken its name; it was the sailors who also made women known to him; he responded with nausea and intoxication, from which sprang his burning voyeur's curiosity about all things erotic. Indeed, it was through women that he began to falsify the world; from what he saw, sensed, and surmised about women he drew the materials that led him to an inexhaustible and, with time, flawless fantasticating. It was definitely through women, through the fantasy that he had conceived of women, that he had created his fantasy of the Arab world to which the language and customs of his country, and, obscurely, also his own blood, attracted him. "Only the things of fantasy are beautiful. And memory, too, is a fantasy…Malta is nothing but a poor, harsh island and the people are as barbarous as when St. Paul was shipwrecked there. Only, being in the sea, it allows imagination to venture into a fable of the Moslem and Christian world, as I have done, as I have been able to do…Others would say history, but I say fable."

Chapter XVI

It was two o'clock in the morning when the Conversation Club on the Piazza Marina received, perhaps from one of the judges, the text of the sentence, which had been scribbled on the back of an envelope. The trial had been held behind closed doors, and soldiers with bayonets at the ready had prevented even small crowds from forming outside the Tribunal. It was known, however, that counsel's arguments had lasted for hours, from two in the afternoon until ten at night, especially because of the energetic pleas entered by Paolo and Gaspare Leone in defense of Di Blasi, and by Felice Firraloro for the other defendants. Talking to the wind, of course, but the Leones in particular insisted because a colleague was involved.

The Marquis of Villabianca seized the envelope; everyone present acknowledged that to do so was his right, knowing how useful it would be for his diary. He began to read aloud: *"Iste Franciscus Paulus Di Blasi decapitetur absque pompa, et ante executionem sententiae torqueatur tamquam cadaver in capite alieno ad vocandos complices, et isti Julius Tinagiia, Benedictus La Villa, et Bernardus Palumbo supendatur in furcis altioribus donec eorum anima e corpore separetur, et executio pro omnibus fiat in planitie divae Theresiae extra Porta Nuova…"*

The rest of the sentence was lost, drowned by a torrent of comments, questions, and explanations. Everyone was satisfied, but not because the sentence was so exemplary – it could not have been other than what it was, given the crime and the need to impress Jacobins and plebeians alike with the power of the State; they were content because Di Blasi – a man who belonged to their class, after all – had been granted decapitation, the Court thus setting him apart from his accomplices, who were to be hanged.

The waiters, who threaded a frenetic zigzag among the tables bearing iced drinks, *scorzonere,* and Neapolitan ices, mentally addressed each lady or gentleman they served with a "May it refresh your—!" or "May it refresh your cuckold's horns!" and hurried back to the kitchen, where their co-workers were busy setting up orders and commenting pithily on the satisfaction of their masters.

"They're pleased that he won't hang but'll have his head chopped off!"

"We serve the iced drinks, they guzzle them…The rope for us, the axe for them."

"You think that's such a great advantage? The pleasure of having your head chopped off—"

"It's the difference between a meal with meat and a meal of plain dried beans."

"No, it's not a difference in kind, it's a difference in style."

"Some style! Myself, I'd rather keep my body in one piece.

The idea of being stuffed into a coffin in two pieces would make me sick."

"How would you know you were in two pieces?"

"My soul would know it."

"Your soul doesn't think. It gets ready to be roasted and it looks."

"Looks at what?"

"At the filthy business life is…or at the emptiness that comes later and that is nothing but emptiness."

"All the same, with the knife you die fast. Even in a thing like this, they come off better than we do."

"But he's left without his head!"

The same question as to whether, style aside, the guillotine was superior to the gallows was being debated by the Countess di Regalpetra, Don Saverio Zarbo, and the Marquis di Villanova.

"Say what you like, but one's head, dear Lord, one's head!…" the Marquis was saying, and he touched his neck as if to make sure his own was well attached.

"I would never have supposed that it mattered to you so much," Don Saverio said, never able to resist a gibe.

"It mattered to *him*," the Countess said.

"That he should present us with this fine distinction in style, you mean?" the Marquis asked.

"No, do you know what I think?" Don Saverio asked. "That *he*, as the Countess says" – he emphasized the pronoun by way of allusion to the past connections of the Countess and Di Blasi – "that he will actually suffer more from the distinction *heartless*

the Court has granted him … He believed in equality, he fought for it, and now they give him the axe and his companions get the rope."

"Then the sentence is completely just from that point of view as well. In a case like this, the punishment should contain the opposite of the ideas of which the accused has been found guilty," the Marquis said.

"Exactly," said Don Saverio.

"Who knows what he's thinking at this moment. He must be so – so disheartened. I do feel so sorry for him. I'm afraid I shan't shut my eyes all night long," the Countess said.

"I do believe that," Don Saverio said.

"May I recommend something? An infusion of hearts of lettuce, a cupful, a good cupful, and you'll sleep like an angel," the Marquis said.

"Really? But a broth of lettuce hearts must have a horrid taste. I don't think I could drink a whole cup."

"Add a touch of lemon," Don Saverio advised.

Chapter XVII

Every day Father Teresi came to visit him: the attention was probably a request of Monsignor Airoldi's, but it was not much appreciated by the Abbot. He knew that Teresi was not only the chaplain of the Castellammare prison, but also the spy of Monsignor López: dog does not eat dog, well enough, but he found it distasteful just to look at the man and that meek expression of his, which would persuade anyone to hand his heart over into the priest's keeping. However, after seventeen days in jail, the Abbot's distaste began to fade from habit, not to overlook the fact that Teresi was in a position to do him some favors.

It was from him the Abbot heard that Di Blasi had been sentenced to death and that the penalty would be carried out the next day. "Unless," Teresi added, "the proverb that says the executioner is never absent turns out not to be true."

"Why, what has happened?"

"What's happened is that our honorable hangman Di Martino fell from the top of the gallows while he was setting it up in front of Santa Teresa, so now he's in the Central Hospital and he's not got one whole bone in his body."

"A sign from Fate," the Abbot said.

"What Fate, what Fate? Di Martino is getting on, his strength doesn't match his zeal any more. He needs help—"

"But it will be impossible to carry out the sentence without him."

"It will have to be delayed a few hours maybe, or for a day, but they'll find someone else, never fear."

"I would like to ask you a favor," the Abbot said.

"Anything I can do, believe me. I am at your service, like a brother."

"Thank you...It's this: I should like to say goodbye to Lawyer Di Blasi."

"That, believe me as if I were your own brother, is not possible. He is kept under such strict guard, you'd be appalled."

So that's how a brother acts, the Abbot thought. "But you see him, you talk to him. I am a priest, too."

"It's not the same thing."

I know, you're a spy. Aloud he said, "I understand...But could you at least give him my greetings, tell him—"

"What?" Teresi asked; he was suddenly so eager for the Abbot to tell him something he could pass on to Monsignor López that his ears buzzed.

"Tell him...Well, tell him that I have repented what I did...The codices, you know...Yes, repented, and that I want him to know, and that...Nothing, just that I have repented, and that I send my greetings..."

"What is he, your confessor?"

"No, it's not that...It's complicated, you know, it's devilishly hard to explain." It *is* complicated, he thought, because it's not true at all that I'm sorry. And by telling him that I am, it isn't that I want to deceive him. Or even to comfort him, because it doesn't really matter to him about me or the codices, and of all times, not now. It's that...

"I'll tell him. And I can do more than that. In a little while they'll be taking him away for more torture—"

"More?"

"The sentence says '*torqueatur tamquam cadaver in capite aliena ad vocandos complices*.' You can take your walk on the roof earlier than usual, I'll tell the guards, and if you keep to the side that looks out over the main courtyard, you'll see him on his way to the carriage. I'll tell him that you'll be on the roof, and that he should look up. As a matter of fact, I'll go this minute."

"I will be very much obliged to you," the Abbot said, "and don't forget to tell him what I told you."

A quarter of an hour later, the guards came to fetch him for his walk. The sun was blindingly bright, and for a moment the Abbot's head swam. Then he felt as free and light as the flag with its fleur-de-lis which rustled above his head and snapped when the wind blew in from the sea. Down in the courtyard the carriage was waiting, black as a sarcophagus against the shining gravel. The Abbot opened his breviary and pretended to read. He said to himself that what he was doing was stupid and even ridiculous, like everything dictated by feeling, which has meaning only in the sphere of emotion but is grotesque in reality. Yet he was anxious and moved, his whole being tense with expectation.

Perhaps no more than a half hour passed: four soldiers crossed the courtyard toward the carriage; behind them, walking slowly and with difficulty between two other soldiers, came Francesco Paolo Di Blasi. The distance and the slanting light made the figures moving across the courtyard look shrunken, no taller than the shadows they cast. But when he came to the carriage and a soldier held open the door, Di Blasi seemed to grow to his full stature once more. He turned and looked up toward the roof. Then he lifted his hat and bowed slightly. The Abbot was gripped by terror and horror: the man down below who was bowing to him had white hair. His black clothing, the black carriage, the black shadows threw that utterly unexpected white head into terrible relief.

The Abbot could not distinguish his features, but under that white hair the face seemed wizened, desiccated. He replied to the bow by waving his breviary. Di Blasi disappeared into the carriage. The stunned, lingering silence was split by the coachman's voice, and the wheels clattered over the gravel.

"My God," the Abbot murmured. "God, my God."

Never had he confronted life with such terror. He remembered stories about malevolent phantoms, about people whose hair suddenly turned gray at their appearance; Di Blasi had seen living men turn into malignant phantoms.

Teresi came up a few minutes later to bring him Di Blasi's reply, and found the Abbot leaning on the parapet; he was ashen, and his eyes were wild and vacant.

"Do you feel ill?" the priest asked.

"The sun," said the Abbot. "I have a slight sunstroke, my head aches."

"Let us go down," Teresi said, and took his arm.

Perhaps it really was the sun, the Abbot thought. He wanted to be quit of that vision, that memory. He did not even want to know whether the Chaplain had delivered his message to Di Blasi. But – "I told him what you wanted me to tell him," Teresi said.

The Abbot stared at him blankly.

"He answered," the Chaplain continued, "that there is so much fraud in life, and that yours has at least the merit of being a zestful one, and even, in one sense, as he put it, useful. And that he admires your imagination."

"He said that?"

"Those very words. And he hopes that you will soon be at liberty again, and he sends you his greetings."

"They will torture him again, you said?"

"Yes, but it will be simply *pro forma*, I think. His feet are like overripe pomegranates; the doctor says it would be too risky to use any more fire… What was I saying? Oh, yes. The sentence will be carried out tomorrow at the specified time. They appealed to the prisoners in the Vicaría for a volunteer executioner, a temporary one, and twenty or more responded. They've chosen one – a bull of a man, I can tell you. He had sixteen more years to serve, and he still can't believe his good luck… Yes, yes, the sayings of the ancients always turn out to be true: the executioner is never absent."

Chapter XVIII

He took off his shoes; he felt the relief of the swimmer who surfaces for air only to dive back into the water, for now he had to take off his stockings, which were stuck to his feet with blood and pus. With one terrible decision of will and hand, strip them off – quickly.

The judges turned away and pretended to consult among themselves, so that they would not have to see. Even the police looked somewhere, anywhere else – out the window, up at the ceiling. When they glanced back, Di Blasi was stockingless; his feet leaked a greenish slime.

"Let us get on with this," said one of the judges: the stench of those suppurating feet combined with the smell of fat melting down was turning his stomach. Melted fat, boiling fat was to be the torture device this time rather than direct fire, which, in the doctor's opinion, the prisoner could no longer survive.

"This will be a token application," the presiding judge said, "merely to observe the terms of the sentence."

"Thank you."

"It was the doctor who objected to further torture."

The judge preferred not to accept the thanks of a convicted criminal.

The fat in the kettle was gurgling over the fire. That heavy kitchen odor in a torture chamber helped a little to take his mind off his atrocious pain. There was something ridiculous, grotesque about these men, police and judges alike, hovering over the bubbling oil like women in the kitchen preparing the lard after a slaughtering. For a moment, his mind wandered among recollections of how, as a child, he used to roam the kitchen on days when they were preparing the lard, to nibble on cracklings, which he loved; it was a big kitchen, and in the smoky half light, the copper pots and pans gleamed like small crepuscular suns. It had been years since he had gone into that kitchen or eaten cracklings; the taste and the image were associated with boyhood. A nagging, painful thought crept into this memory: the judges and the police had also had childhoods; perhaps the smell made them remember some long-ago happiness or yearn for the peace and quiet of home; he thought how in a little while the distastefulness of the duty they were carrying out – that is, of torturing a fellow man – would be submerged in sweet, familiar fogs; presently they would eat and sleep and play with their children; they would make love; they would worry over the baby's cold and the dog's distemper; the setting sun, a flight of swallows, the perfume of a garden would move them to sorrow or delight. And now they were witnessing torture. This should not happen to a man, he thought. In the future it would not happen, not in a world enlightened by reason. (What despair would have accompanied his last hours had he had even a presentiment that, in the luminous future he envisaged, whole peoples would devote themselves to torturing others; that men of culture, lovers of music, exemplary family men, men who were kind to animals, would destroy millions of other men with implacable method and bestial skill, that even the most direct heirs of Reason would reintroduce the "question" into the world – no longer as a factor of law, which it was at the moment he endured it, but actually as a factor of existence.)

"Not on the open wounds," the presiding judge said to the policeman who had offered to substitute for poor Di Martino, who at that moment, neglected by doctors and nurses, lay groaning in the Central Hospital on a straw mattress they had thrown down on the floor for him. Like a dog, worse than a dog. The policeman had volunteered because the torture was to be a matter of form, of preserving appearances; he hoped word of it would not get about, for then the already unbearable shame he endured for being a policeman would have added to it the infamy of being a torturer. He would take care not to make the prisoner suffer, so that in all conscience, seconded by the testimony of those present, he could say that he had volunteered precisely so as not to make him suffer, considering the fact that at the hands of someone else he would have suffered; and if one stops to reflect, this is the justification many people adduce for their vocation or profession as torturers. However that may be, he did work with a light hand. He held the receptacle, shaped somewhat like a coffeepot, high, so that the liquid would cool a little as it fell through the air; he tipped the pot slowly to make the oil fall drop by drop on the top of the foot, which was still without lesions and blisters.

Di Blasi was so conditioned to pain that he felt only a sensation like the prickings of a needle. And it did not last more than a minute. When the judge pronounced "That is enough," for the judges his body stopped existing; they consigned the care of his soul to the Confraternity of the Whites.

He was escorted to the military district of San Giacomo, where there were three churches: the Maddalena, San Paolo, and San Giacomo; this last, being the principal one, was chosen for the comfort of the principal prisoner. Corporal Palumbo got San Paolo, Tenaglia and La Villa the Maddalena.

Acting for the Whites, Don Francesco Barlotta, Prince di San Giuseppe, was there to receive Di Blasi and comfort him in his last hours. The Prince was the ideal man for this office; after twenty-four hours spent in his company, one would come to view even death as a welcome release. Di Blasi, who knew the Prince well, was appalled by the prospect of having to discuss eternal verities with him; once they had exchanged the amenities, rather as if they had met on the promenade or in some drawing room, he said firmly that he had several things he wanted to write; he wished to record the emotions and resolutions that these last hours would dictate to him. Actually, he had nothing he wanted to write, but he did want to spend those few hours alone.

The Prince, who had all the arguments of spiritual solace on the tip of his tongue, felt cast down. He had prepared himself very diligently: he had read *The Idiot*, translated into Italian by the Prince di Butera; since it was the month of May, he had also provided himself with a fat volume of *Hebdomanda Mariana*; in dealing with a man who was so knowledgeable about books and so arrogant in his criminality, one would require arguments based on unimpeachable dogma and radiant truth; where better look for these than in the joyous, dolorous, glorious Mysteries of the Most Holy Mary? But with Di Blasi electing to write in solitude, nothing remained for the Prince to do but pray for him, so from another collection he had brought with him he set to reading prayers for mercy, a shriven death, and redemption.

Because he felt that he could not and should not write all the true and profound things that stirred within him, Di Blasi began to write verses. The concept of poetry then prevalent held that the poet is free to lie. Today the concept of poetry no longer permits this, although perhaps poetry itself allows it still.

Chapter XIX

"The Lord God, who sees into the heart of His every creature, sees and judges mine, and to this end I pray unto Him. But I pray above all that He long preserve the well-being of this Kingdom and that he also long preserve and bless Your Holy Royal Majesty, the Queen Consort, and the Family Royal…"

"The well-being of this Kingdom!" Abbot Vella sneered. He laid down his pen and scattered sand over the page. "There, it's done at last. Now Monsignor Airoldi can rest easy." He blew the sand off and arranged the pages in order. He reread them. The best part of the letter, he decided, was where he denied having falsified anything and at the same time covertly admitted that he had:

"One would have to agree that had I done nothing but guess or fantasticate, no one could have guessed more truly or conceived a more lively fantasy; the creator of such a remarkable work would, if I may say so, deserve far greater fame than the humble translator of two Arabic codices…"

In the distance, a scattering of bells began to toll. The Abbot crossed himself and prayed that eternal grace be granted Francesco Paolo Di Blasi. Soon he will be in the world of truth, he thought, and was struck with dismay at the sudden idea that the world of truth might be here and now, in the world of living men, of history, of books.

That same thought, but better rooted and more confident, was with Di Blasi as he stepped up onto the scaffold.

The square was almost deserted; there were only the few faithful souls who would rush forward the instant the execution was over and the corpses removed, to snatch a length of rope or some other reliquary of the "justice" they had just enjoyed; this would become their homeopathic amulet against the hanging they suspected might very likely be awaiting them. Among the few clusters of these obscene, ragged people, the well-dressed, well-brushed, rosy-cheeked Dr. Hager was prominently visible. They want to know everything, see everything, Di Blasi thought, but they fail to see the essentials, the things that really count...And he will write in his diary about my beheading, but he will not write one word about the reasons why they are beheading me. He remembered the spring day when he had accompanied Goethe to Monreale; there was a man who was moved by a potsherd from Hellenic Selinus or by a coin from Syracuse, but who had stood, impassive and almost repelled, before the world-renowned mosaics in the Cathedral.

The scaffold was draped in black; black candles were on hand; presently they would be lighted and set around his dead body. Death had been duly decked out in deference to his station. A servant wearing the mourning livery of the

Di Blasis held in his hand the silver basin into which his master's head would fall. He was the youngest servant in the household; Di Blasi wondered by what trick of persuasion or pressure the others had contrived to saddle him with this sad duty; the boy's eyes were filled with tears and he was shaking as if he had a chill. Not even my mother understood me, not even she was able to read my heart, if now she sends me this wretched liveried boy and a silver basin and black candles.

He walked over to the servant and put a hand on his shoulder. "When the time comes," he said, "shut your eyes."

The boy nodded. Di Blasi turned away, feeling suddenly that he was about to burst into helpless tears.

The executioner stood before him: he was a strapping man, but now he seemed shrunken into himself, uneasy and intimidated. His name was Calogero Gagliano, and he was a goatherd from Girgenti; he had killed a man, and he saw nothing wrong in killing one more, certainly not when it was done in the name of justice and he would thereby obtain an amnesty for the sixteen years he had still to serve. He paid no mind whatever to the others whom he had to hang, but he did feel a twinge of fear at having to cut off a gentleman's head, a lawyer's head. And so he had come up to Di Blasi to stammer, "Your Worship'll forgive me."

"Think of your freedom," the condemned man said, to hearten him.

The Prince di San Giuseppe held out the white silk handkerchief; under his white hood, he began to murmur prayers almost in counterpart with the Chaplain's tenor.

Di Blasi looked around the square for the last time; he saw Dr. Hager again; the man stood watching attentively, as if he were deciphering a page from the Codex of San Martino. The spectators crossed themselves; the executioner crossed himself, and began to pray. He prayed to his God, the God of goats and of the *malocchio*, that he give him a steady hand to cut the rope, that the axe fall true.

And his prayer was heard.

Characters

King   Malta

Benedictine Giuseppe Villa

Viceroy Caracciolo - reformer

Monsignor Airoldi

Francesco Paolo di Blasi -
    aristocratic lawyer

Canon Gregorio

Judge 3rd ⟶ Grassellini

royal patrimony

Monsignor Lopez

Duke of Caccamo - friend

p. 58 more merit in inventing
history (oral culture)
p. 62 it's a game
66 perils of the Council of
Egypt

About the author

il inganno - hoax
la truffa - fraud, swindle,
cheat

Leonardo Sciascia (1921–1983) was a novelist and politician whose works were often set in his troubled, mafia-blighted homeland of Sicily. He hailed from Racalmuto in the southwest of the island and lived there for much of his life.

Vella - forger, storyteller

About the introducer

forces of change becoming irresistable

Michael Schmidt is a critic and poet and editorial and managing director of Carcanet Press. His books include *Lives of the Poets*, several collections of poems, two novels, critical books, and anthologies.

More from Apollo

NOW IN NOVEMBER
Josephine Johnson

> *Now in November I can see our years as a whole. This autumn is like both an end and a beginning to our lives, and those days which seemed confused with the blur of all things too near and too familiar are clear and strange now.*

Forced out of the city by the Depression, Arnold Haldmarne moves his wife and three daughters to the country and tries to scratch a living from the land. After years of unrelenting hard work, the hiring of a young man from a neighbouring farm upsets the fragile balance of their lives. And in the summer, the rains fail to come.

BOSNIAN CHRONICLE
Ivo Andrić

> *For as long as anyone could remember, the little café known as 'Lutvo's' has stood at the far end of the Travnik bazaar, below the shady, clamorous source of the 'Rushing Brook'.*

This is a sweeping saga of life in Bosnia under Napoleonic rule. Set in the remote town of Travnik, the newly appointed French consul soon finds himself intriguing against his Austrian rival, whilst dealing with a colourful cast of locals.

THE MAN WHO LOVED CHILDREN
Christina Stead

> *All the June Saturday afternoon Sam Pollit's children were on the lookout for him as they skated round the dirt sidewalks and seamed old asphalt of R Street and Reservoir Road that bounded the deep-grassed acres of Tohoga House, their home.*

Sam and Henny Pollit have too many children, too little money and too much loathing for each other. As Sam uses the children's adoration to feed his own voracious ego, Henny becomes a geyser of rage against her improvident husband.

MY SON, MY SON
Howard Spring

> *What a place it was, that dark little house that was two rooms up and two down, with just the scullery thrown in! I don't remember to this day where we all slept, though there was a funeral now and then to thin us out.*

This is the powerful story of two hard-driven men – one a celebrated English novelist, the other a successful Irish entrepreneur – and of their sons, in whom are invested their fathers' hopes and ambitions. Oliver Essex and Rory O'Riorden grow up as friends, but their fathers' lofty plans have unexpected consequences as the violence of the Irish Revolution sweeps them all into uncharted territory.

DELTA WEDDING
Eudora Welty

> *The nickname of the train was the Yellow Dog. Its real name was the Yazoo-Delta. It was a mixed train. The day was the 10th of September, 1923 – afternoon. Laura McRaven, who was nine years old, was on her first journey alone.*

Laura McRaven travels down the Delta to attend her cousin Dabney's wedding. At the Fairchild plantation her family envelop her in a tidal wave of warmth, teases and comfort. As the big day approaches, tensions inevitably rise to the surface.

THE DAY OF JUDGMENT
Salvatore Satta

> *At precisely nine o'clock, as he did every evening, Don Sebastiano Sanna Carboni pushed back his armchair, carefully folded the newspaper which he had read through to the very last line, tidied up the little things on his desk, and prepared to go down to the ground floor…*

Around the turn of the twentieth century, in the isolated Sardinian town of Nuoro, the aristocratic notary Don Sebastiano Sanna reflects on his life, his family's history and the fortunes of this provincial backwater where he has lived out his days. Written over the course of a lifetime and published posthumously, *The Day of Judgment* is a classic of Italian, and world, literature.

THE AUTHENTIC DEATH OF HENDRY JONES
Charles Neider

> *Nowadays, I understand, the tourists come for miles to see Hendry Jones' grave out on the Punta del Diablo and to debate whether his bones are there or not…*

A stark and violent depiction of one of America's most alluring folk heroes, the mythical, doomed gunslinger. Set on the majestic coast of southern California, Doc Baker narrates his tale of the Kid's capture, trial, escape and eventual murder. Written in spare and subtle prose, this is one of the great literary treatments of America's obsession with the rule of the gun.

THE LOST EUROPEANS
Emanuel Litvinoff

> *Coming back was worse, much worse, than Martin Stone had anticipated.*

Martin Stone returns to the city from which his family was driven in 1938. He has concealed his destination from his father, and hopes to win some form of restitution for the depressed old man living in exile in London. *The Lost Europeans* portrays a tense, ruined yet flourishing Berlin where nothing is quite what it seems.

THE STONE ANGEL

Margaret Laurence

> *Above the town, on the hill brow, the stone angel used to stand.*
> *I wonder if she stands there yet…*

Hagar Shipley has lived a quiet life full of rage. As she approaches her death, she retreats from the squabbling of her son and his wife to reflect on her past – her ill-advised marriage, her two sons, the harshness of life on the prairie, her own failures and the failures of others.

HEAVEN'S MY DESTINATION

Thornton Wilder

> *One morning in the late summer of 1930 the proprietor and several guests at the Union Hotel at Crestcrego, Texas, were annoyed to discover Biblical texts freshly written across the blotter on the public writing-desk.*

George Marvin Brush is a travelling textbook salesman and fervent religious convert, determined to lead the godless to a better life. With sad and sometimes hilarious consequences, his travels will take him into the soul of 1930s America.

THE HISTORY OF A TOWN
M.E. Saltykov-Shchedrin

> *The town-governors… all flogged the inhabitants, but the first*
> *flogged them pure and simple, the second explained their zeal…*
> *and the third asked only that in all matters the inhabitants should*
> *trust in their valour.*

One of the major satirical novels of the 19th century, Shchedrin's farcical history of Glupov follows the bewildered and stoical Russian inhabitants for hundreds of years as they endure the violence and lunacy of their tyrannical rulers.

THE HUNGRY GRASS
Richard Power

> *At the funeral, several priests remarked how appropriate it was that*
> *Father Conroy should have returned on his last day to Rosnagree,*
> *the parish in which he was born.*

Father Tom Conroy – a spiky, difficult man – dies at a reunion of his seminary colleagues. In this sharp, witty and moving novel, we are taken through the years that formed this troublesome priest, who knew his life had been a failure.

vizioso – vicious
feroce – fierce, savage
sadico – sadistic